TUMOUR–DJINN

By Zoltan Komor

FOR

MorbidBookS. Wordpress.Com

TUMOUR–DJINN

MALL-HEAD

THE NOISE OF construction wakes me up in the morning. Turning to my side, I notice that a yellow string cordons off my sleeping wife. There's a tiny excavator on her forehead, and one inch long workers are demolishing her face with concrete crushers. A black sign on the yellow line says: WIFE UNDER CONSTRUCTION.

Great, she must have ordered this one too from her favourite online beauty shop, no matter how much I keep telling her, she doesn't need any of these stuff. I watch as a crane lowers my wife's new nose into the dug out red pit in the center of her face. It's quite a pretty nose, I admit. A few smudgy workers hammer her face using all of their strength, the others are just sitting on her ear, drinking beer. One even stands up and pisses down onto the pillow.

There's a little guy holding a piece of paper. That must be the blueprint. I peek over the tiny man's shoulder, and gaze at the drawing. Say! It looks rather nice! But it could be better. Using two fingers, I pinch out the blueprint from the guy's hands. He yells at me, shaking his micro fist, but I flick him away. Then I sneak out to the kitchen, holding a magnifying glass and a very sharp pencil I make a few changes in the drawing. Then another few. Making the nose look a bit thinner, the forehead more narrow, and so on. When I'm done, I hand back the blueprint to the little guy, who seemingly tries to kill me with his needle-point eyes.

After a few hours, they finish the job. A man dressed in a suit arrives; he cuts the string with scissors, drinks a few glasses of champagne, then staggers back to a matchbox sized limousine he arrived in. He drives away, disappearing behind the closet.

I hardly recognize my wife, she is so beautiful. Other people stare at her too. In the street, tourists come over to us, they ask if they could photo themselves with my wife's face. A telephone call arrives: a noted international architectural magazine would like to publish a picture of her head. After a week, they send us a copy. Her portrait is on the forth page, along with a newly built shopping mall in Yokohama. I keep praising myself for making those changes in the blueprint. But then, the accident happens: on a windy day, walking on the street, a strange noise arrives from my wife's head, a cracking sound, like if something collapsed behind her eyebrows. A little piece of her forehead falls out, down to the pavement, and through the hole, I can see the wrinkled brain in the skull. Whats more, one of her eyeballs slackens, it seems like, it might pop out from it's socket any minute. When she gazes down, you can clearly see the muscle-line that holds the eye in it's place. She looks pretty awful. I keep consoling her, wiping her hanging, crying eyeball with a hanky, telling her, one of the miniature workers must have fucked up the blueprint.

So we order the face-reconstruction beauty pack again. I lay my wife in bed, and open the package. Tiny workers crawl out, and pester her face. I take away their blueprint, and show them the opened architectural magazine. They look at it, scratching their chins, then they nod and begin to work. Seemingly, they want to start from scratch – they slide tiny dynamite sticks into her face dimples, they run into shelter. Soon, an explosion tears my wife's head into bloody pieces of meat – and then construction begins. I feel tired. A fall asleep, leaving them to work.

In the morning, waking up I find the miniature version of the shopping mall in Yokohama in the place of my wife's head.

"好き?" she asks, her voice echoes through the small building along with calming music. Tiny Japanese teenagers with party-coloured hair wander around behind her window-eyes. They wave to me, then venture into a sushi bar.

THE WILD BULL

Inspired by the electronic music piece of Morton Subotnick

COBBLES HEATED UP by the sun – like the thousand shoulder-blades of the devil. Above the narrow street hangs a bunch of dead roosters on a drying-line. Red ink keeps dripping out from their cut throats down, to the by-passers heads. Stray dogs stick their long tongues into dark puddles. Children in raunchy trousers run up and down in the morning hot-spell, begging for money on the corners.

"For one peso, I'll show you, what's today's bullfight gonna be like!" offers a dirty faced boy to a fat tourist, who hands him a coin.

"It'd better be good!" he warns the kid, who begins to shadow play. His small hands shield a tiny man and a bull onto the cracked wall. The animal rushed towards the tiny toreador, who steps aside in the final moment, and tricks the bull.

"I say! I can't believe it! Like it was real!" the fat fellow wonders, touching the wall with his sausage fingers.

"Stop! Don't do it, senor!" shouts the boy, but it is too late. The little shadow-bull runs at the groping hand, stabbing its horns deep into the skin. The tourist's scream echoes through the streets, it lights the cigars between the chapped lips in the boozer, where sweaty men place their bets and glasses clink. Not far, in the arena the wood benches creak as the first arrivers take their seats.

The toreador is still at home, standing in front of the mirror, putting on his glittering clothes. Then he steps into the bedroom, and pulls off the red blanket from his naked lover. Her milk-white skin almost lights in the shady room.

"I'm gonna sit in the first line, like always!" she promises. "Will you give me the bull's testicles?"

"You little eager!" The toreador smiles and fondles the girl's face. Then he runs out of the room, holding the blanket.

Distant trumpets harrumph and fat, raddled faced senoras arrive. Their gigantic boobs sway left to right and right to left, knocking off the plaster from the walls. Men turn and whistle after them. But then, the admirers notice that these aren't real women at all, only shadow figures.

"Come here, you skunk!" they yell at the dirty faced boy, who begins to laugh, and runs toward the alley, with the angry men in his back.

"Now this is what I call running of the bulls!" the kid cheers, accidentally knocking over a basket full of apples. The boy disappears behind the next corner, but his shadow stays behind, picking up the shadows of the fruits, putting them into the shade of the basket.

The toreador stands now in the middle of the arena, facing the corral's wooden door, shaken by the attacks of a wild animal in the other side. Tears of sweat keep dripping from his moustache to the thirsty ground. He turns aside, and watches his lover, as she sends a kiss to him. The kiss turns into a white pigeon in the air. Men in black hats arrive and try to catch the scared bird that flies above their stretching fingers, then sits on to the toreador's shoulder. But then, the trumpets begin to cry, scaring away the bird that disappears in the sky. A sharp slam shakes the air, as the corral door swings open, knocking down the plaster from the old wall of the arena. The toreador stretches his muscles, and the crowd rumbles. As the smoke of the plaster dust subsides, the toreador's mouth hangs open, when he sees, that there is no bull in the corral, only a small, dirty faced boy stands there. What a joke, he was the one, who banged the door with an old, rusty bucket. The crowd begins to laugh, and the toreador tries to join them, but only flustered whimpers leaves his throat. The red blanket shakes in his hand.

"Senor, senor, I can invoke the beast if you like, it will only cost you one peso!" cheers the boy, dropping the bucket. He twists his fingers, and a shadow-bull appears on the wall.

"Here's your enemy, mister! Come quick, or it will run away in fear!"

The toreador just stands there, ashamed, the red blanket falls into the dust. He looks at the crowd with supplicant eyes, but everyone just keeps laughing. Then he stares at his lover. She's the only one, who doesn't even smile. She just sits there with a straight face; her jaws keep chewing, like she was eating something. What can it be? There's some kind of bloody egg between her fingers. The legs of the toreador begin to shake. As he looks down, he sees a growing blood stain on his trousers, between his legs. He faints and collapses into the ground. His shadow flies out from under him, and moves into the small boy's palm.

*

The cables melt quietly under the soft steps of the girl. As she walks over the narrow streets, her white dress and even more whiter skin fades into the walls. Suddenly a hand taps her back. She turns around, and sees a small beggar boy. The dust on his young face is like a shadow.

"Senorita!" begins the kid. "For one peso, I'll show you, what's today's bullfight gonna be like!"

The girl begins to laugh hearing this offer; she tousles the youngster's hair.

"Don't bother, I know exactly what it's gonna be like!" she answers. "It's gonna be glorious! You can believe me, I'm the toreador's lover! And he's a real hero, who already defeated ninety-nine bulls! He told me, when he conquers this one too, he's gonna hire a psychic to invoke the ghosts of the hundred bulls, just to fight them again!"

Then she leaves the kid, who follows her with his angry eyes. As the girl walks away, she suddenly feels a raindrop hitting her shoulder. Then another one and another one came. Is it going to rain? That would be a real disaster, because the bullfight would be cancelled, and she couldn't watch her beautiful lover fighting his hundredth bull. She looks up, and realizes, that these aren't raindrops at all. Dead roosters hang above the street on drying-lines, the blood keep dripping from their cut throats.

"Oh, my pretty white dress!" she hisses, looking at the red dots on her shoulder. Then she hears that the boy behind him begins to laugh. The girl continue to walk, the blood keeps dripping on her. Where ever she looks, she sees dead roosters – they are everywhere, hundreds of them, hanging on those strings. More and more tears fall on her, it's almost like a blood rain that slowly paints her dress all red. The girl finally decides to turn back. She gives the boy a bitter look. He just stands there, still laughing.

"Stop it!" she yells at the kid. The dress and her skin are all red now. The girl begins to cry.

"I would hurry up a bit, if I were you, Senorita!" tells the boy. "They will soon release the bull. I bet that beast gonna like your new dress very much!"

She opens her mouth, and tries to answer, when a sharp slam of a door shakes the air, and the knocking of hooves can be heard. The red girl begins to run, she gasps and yells for help, but it seems like the whole city would be empty.

"Maybe everyone's at the arena!" the thought crosses her mind, accidentally knocking over a basket full of apples. She runs along, speeding up, turning right in the next corner – almost hearing the huffs of the bull behind her. She's afraid to look back.

The next street is just like the exact copy of the previous one. And then, every street looks the same. A bowed over basket and rolled away apples hampers her everywhere.

*

Moustached men keep blowing their golden trumpets – the crowing of roosters fills the arena – the sound of horned pigeons vibrate in the air – the whimpers of stray dogs under the hot cobbles. The toreador cuts out his image from the mirror with a sharp sword. He hands it to her lover, who kisses it all over, painting it red with her rouged lips. Later, the man steps into the plaza de toros, and watches as his mirror image wilts into a shadow between his fingers.

"You aren't gonna defeat the bull with that, senor!" yells a fuzzy haired little boy from the crowd. The people around him begin to howl.

The walls sweat, salty drops on the lime, like the shiny tears of the old building. Young girls tear off their kissing mouths, and throw them at the toreador, who dribbles the squelching lips with the shadow in his hand.

"Toro!" he laughs. The crowd gets excited, they pass around a basket full of apples, and everyone takes out one fruit. They begin to peg them at the toreador, who skilfully sidesteps from the flying apples.

"Toro! Toro!" he yells, strutting up and down, like a shiny rooster, provoking the human mass. Someone throws the empty basket at him, but he jumps away, and it lands on the ground. His lover in the first line moans in pleasure, admiring his man's skills.

Soon huddle rises. The dirty faced boy is the spokesman, he's tiny, but cruel voice echoes int he arena: "Stone him!"

So the people run out to the streets, and pry out the hot cobbles, which they begin to throw at the running toreador.

"Leave him alone!" his lover begs to them, white pigeons fly out from her throat, but no use, the villagers kick and squelch the birds with their boots.

The ashes of smouldered horns all over the town got spread. Glasses hustle in the boozer. Dogs lie in the shadows of fat Senoras. The girl stands in the street, looking up at her dead lover, who hangs above the narrow street, on a drying-line. Blood keep dripping from his wounds, painting the girl's white dress and face all red, the drops mix with her shinny tears.

"See, Senorita, it's your entire fault!" tells the boy behind her. "If you would have given me that peso, I would have showed you, this is going to happen."

Then the bigger boy walks away, the alleys drink up his long echoing laugh. The girl bends down and pries out the toreador's shadow from the ground. She crosses it over her hand, and returns home. There she lies in her bed, blanket her with the shadow, and closes her eyes. A nightmare rushes at her forehead over and over again.

TUMOUR-DJINN

I ORDER A magic lamp from the internet. According to the seller, it is good as new, and after rubbing the thing, a djinn will come out and give me three wishes. A few days pass, and the package arrives. A sign on the lamp's side informs me that the product is not suitable for children under the age of three, because they can swallow the small pieces. I don't know what tiny parts a genie could possibly have, but nowadays they write this warning to everything.

I begin to rub the lamp, but what comes out fails to meet even my lowest expectations. Along with some dark smoke a thin, bald guy crawls out. His skin is all grey, the eyes are colorless pebbles. He hands me his medical charts, like it was a business card or something, which reads: Stage 4 Lung Cancer.

"I never smoked one cigarette in my life!" adds the genie, and begins to cough.

I don't know what to do with my new cancerous djinn. I keep telling him my wishes, but he just stares in silence, or talks about nonsense.

"I want a tree which grows money as leaves!" I command him.

"I never realized, life can be so short. We are just putting the bricks, one into another, then we try to climb over the wall that we created. But it is so big. It covers the sun." he mutters, drawing in the air with his pencil-like fingers.

"I want a sports car!" I try again, but he just looks out in the window, gazing the clouds, telling me: "Can cancer grow in birds? Does it kill owls in the forest, or eagles in the mountains? The deer maybe? The giant fish on the bottom of the sea?"

With a desperate look I say: "I want a swimming pool."

But the djinn begins to cough up blood, and it is damned sure, I won't get any swimming pool today.

*

Days pass, the bitter smell of death fills my apartment. My djinn would need a treatment in a hospital, but I can't find his Health Insurance Card inside the magic lamp. So I tell him we are fucked. I brew some chamomile tea, and read a few articles about methods of shrinking a tumour. They say acupuncture can work wonders, so I begin stitching his air with a safety-pin, to activate his inner energy and self-healing abilities. But he looks worse, if that's even possible.

All right, enough, I decide to make a complaint to the seller. I write him an e-mail, telling all about the state of my djinn's health; I even threaten him that I will give a bad rating on the online auction site, if he doesn't take the lamp back. This, of course, is effective: a couple of hours later he answers – offering to send me a new one, if I return him the old.

I spend the rest of the day squeezing the sick djinn back to the tiny oil lamp. He wails and moans in pain, as I keep trying, the bones in his body cracks loudly then he coughs up blood. I realize, it isn't going to work.

"I wish you would go to hell!" I tell him tiredly, catching my breath.

And he says: "I dreamt about woods. Every tree was a year from my life. I was shocked, how big the forest was. I was lost, and walked for hours. Then night came. I knew, I'll never get out of there. So I chopped out the most beautiful years of my life, and made a fire. Moving close to the flames, I wasn't cold nor afraid of the dark anymore."

"Oh, shut up!" I sigh.

*

Eventually, I gave up trying to post back the genie. I leave him laying in my bed, drinking his chamomile tea. Still, the new magic lamp arrives. I realize, that with a fully functional djinn I could solve this whole situation. I unpackage the lamp excitedly. It looks same as the other. So I rub it with a worried look on my face, afraid that this will too puke out another cancerous ghost.

Smoke rises from the lamp. It fills the room, then the whole house. The sick djinn in the bedroom begins to cough louder. And when the dark mist clears, there stands my brand new jinnee, with blue skin, wearing a brown trench coat. A weird smile widens on his hairy face.

He looks quite healthy, which of course encourages me. I'm already thinking about my first wish. I know, if I would cure my first djinn, I could wish three from him too, so totally, I would have five more wishes. Therefore I order my new djinn: "I want you to cure the genie in the other room!"

But nothing happens. My new ghost just lounges there, sending me kisses, then he opens his coat. He's nude under it. His erect penis points directly at me.

"If you rub my magic lamp, you can wish anything you like!" He winks at me, licking his lips. That puts the lid on it! A pervert djinn!

"I want eternal life…" I keep trying, with a shaky voice, but then, the ghost begins to slide his foreskin back and forth on his blue shaft. I gave up.

*

My life turns to hell. Everywhere I go, I run into the pervert genie. He's winking from the kitchen corner, licking his dark, purple lips, staring me through the keyhole, when I lock myself into the bathroom. Showing me dirty photos about himself, laying on a sofa, wearing only women's stockings, his legs are spread, sticking the magic lamp up in his ass. But soon, he realises, I'm just a waste of time. He begins to molest the sick djinn in the bed – sliding his hands under the blanket, telling the ghost, he can cure his cancer, if he rubs his magic lamp between his legs. But no use, the cancerous djinn just stares into the nothing, like he doesn't care about anything anymore. So I became the pervert's primary target again.

No matter, where I hide, he finds me – he drags me out from the closet, pulls me out from under the bed. I run out of the good hiding places very fast. In my final despair, I try to hide in the sick djinn's magic lamp. I know it's a stupid idea, but hearing the pervert djinn's moans and groans getting closer tells me, I figure that it's worth a try.

First, my leg dusappears in the oil lamp. My flesh turns into dark mist in front of my very own eyes. The smoke floats in the room for a while, and the lamp slurps it. Then this happens with all the other parts of my body. Like an ink-drop in the water, I wreathe, then sink into the depths of the old lamp.

*

Hearing the whispers of the wind, I wake up in a forest. Sunshine glitters between the branches, warming up my skin. Fallen leaves crackle as I stand up. But soon, I realise they aren't leaves at all but money – there are banknotes everywhere. They line up on the limbs of the trees too, swaying back and forth in the wind, some fell off, and drifts to the ground.

The forest is composed of money trees, just like the one I was asking for. I begin to pick them up, not believing my luck, filling my pocket with cash. I am rich. I run to one of the trees, and begin to shake it's trunk, showering in money.

TUMOUR–DJINN

*

I'm wandering up and down in the woods with my clothes stuffed with cash. Banknotes crack inside my pants, as I walk. I just traipse for miles and for hours, like a lonely forest ghost, trying to find a way out of the lamp, without any luck. Soon, nightfall slurps up the shadows of the trees, and it becomes clear, that I have to spend the night in this wilderness. It's not a very pleasant thought. I'm both thirsty and hungry – but I can't find a creek nor any berries. Now and again, I hear movement behind some money bushes, but can't get a glimpse at the animals.

The air gets cold, and the sun disappears behind the trees. I'm hitting some stones together, trying to set alight a mound of money. I struggle with this for an hour, hurting my hand, before finally a spark bites into the paper. The money burns away too fast, I have to throw new and new handful of cash into the yellow flames. My belly keeps rumbling, so I try to take the edge off my appetite with some banknotes. It's a bad idea. The dry paper makes me more thirsty.

I curse myself for crawling into the lamp and for wanting a money tree. I look up to the dark sky, searching for stars, but I can only see some sparking gold coins. And I hear movement again from the bushes.

There must be animals around, and I'm going to kill one, I decide, then I fall asleep.

Waking up in the morning, I begin to search for shaft or anything, I can use for hunting. Seeking trough the fallen money-leaves my fingers hitch into a massive, heavy wood handle. Raising it from the papers, it turns out to be an axe. Maybe a lumberjack left it here. Maybe there are other people in this world. Or maybe it belonged to my djinn, who knows. I don't have any energy to think.

*

Tripping along in the thick woods, money branches slap me in the face, as I try to make a way with my axe trough some bushes. I come across a damaged, fallen over sports car. It has crushed like a concertina when it wrecked into a giant money tree, I assume, long time ago. Everything is dusty inside, as I search the vehicle for water or food. But not finding anything, I continue my journey, and after a few minutes, I come upon a clearing. My eyes go wide, when I glimpse the swimming pool. It's gigantic, about 30 metres long and 6 metres wide – like the one I always wanted. The only flaw is the stale water in it – it's a dark, smelly puddle, looks like it wasn't changed for a long, long time ago. But still, it's water for the thirsty. I run over, kneeling down to the white tile I drink, knowing, that I'm surely going to feel sick after this rotten water. Suddenly, I hear a noise. Looking up I see a deer in the other side of the pool. It leans over the water, drinking. My fingers dance on the handle of the axe, sizing up my chances.

TUMOUR–DJINN

Maybe if I come round, I could surprise it from behind. I never hunted before.

*

There's something wrong about this deer. I'm trying to be as quiet as possible, but I move rather clumsily, making a lot of noise. The animal raises it's head, and repeatedly sways it from left to right, but still, it doesn't run away. When I got closer, and it turns towards me, I realize why the animal didn't escaped. The deer is blind. Only two silver coins gleam where it's eyes should be. This encourages me, so I jump forward, raising the axe, and I hit the animal in the head. It staggers, but doesn't fall. The deer springs to my left, trying to escape, but I hit it again, so hard, that the weapon sticks in it's back. The deer takes a few steps forward then back, and finally, it collapses next to the swimming pool.

Looking at the defeated animal, I'm proud of myself. Pulling out my axe, I begin to chop up the carcass. I can almost feel the taste of the meat. But as I cut into it's body, and pull out it's insides, only wet pieces of money streams out of the wound. Widening the hole, I dig deeper, but still, there's nothing in the animal apart from cash. I'm about to curse the skies, when my stomach begins to hurt. I puke out the rotten water.

*

When I glimpse the giant blue penis stretching to the clouds; I can't believe my eyes. I blame the thirst, the hunger and the rotten water for this hallucination. But the pulsating prick won't disappear. Getting closer, I see it grows out of the ground, like the other trees, but it's almost like a mammoth compared to them. A vein throbs in it's side, the cockhead touches the sky. A harsh, masculine odor fills the air. And I can think only about one thing: Meat! Finally, meat!

In the next moment, I'm swinging my axe, like I was cutting a tree, the blade slams into the penis-trunk. A wound appears, blood oozes down to the ground, another bang, and it spurts on me, but I keep going, until I cut a small piece of meat out of it.

Meat! Real meat! I run, and begin to search for rocks. Sparks. Flames. Using the axe as prod, I cook the flesh. Night falls. As I take bite after bite out of the food, coin-eyed deer stick their heads out of the bushes, listening, as I chew. And the sky begins to thunder.

*

It is going to rain. I drop my food and take off my shirt immediately, ready to have a shower. I stand there, opening my mouth wide, waiting for the heavenly fluid to run down on my throat. The blind deer around me gets nervous, and they try to find a shelter under a tree. And then, the rain begins to fall: sharp pieces of metal knock against my forehead. Like tiny asteroids, silver coins pour on me, so hard, that they cut my skin. I scream and run toward the giant penis, which stands a bit slantwise since I chopped a piece out of it. Until I get there, the moneybullets keep hitting my back.

Silvery sounds fill the night, harmonizing with the crying of the deers.

*

Waking up in the morning, I realize, I can't move. The erection of the giant penis has ended – shrunk, it lays on it's side, like a giant blue snail. And on me, pressing me into the ground, squeezing out the life off my body. I bet it brought down a big mount of trees too. I try to crawl out, but it is too heavy. If it gets hard again, I can loose free – it's my only option. But I have no idea when that is going to happen. I squirm from left to right, trying to stimulate the dick with my whole body, but without any effect. Of course, I'm too little, to induce a sky-high hard on. So I wait. And wait some more. The minutes go slow, the hours follow. Sometimes, the waves of panic washes away my thoughts; other times, deadly calm settles upon me. When half a day passes, I begin to worry. A new, frightening idea crosses my head. What if I made it impotent with my axe?

*

I have read once, that a normal guy has about eleven erections a day, not counting the hard ons he has during sleep. Considering that almost a day passed without any movement, it is safe to say, this prick became impotent.

I'm running out of air. Just to wet my dry throat, I'm licking the salty sweat on the skin of the penis, but of course, it just makes me even more thirsty. I know I haven't got much time left. I'm gonna die here, under a fat blue penis, in the middle of a forest, where money grows on trees, and coins rain from the sky. It is very disappointing. I didn't imagine richness to be like this. But if this is the case, I try my best to prepare myself for death. Organize some stuff in the skull-attic. What a mess. Spiderweb covers everything. Old junk everywhere, the decayed relics of childhood, ladders that cannot reach the moon, rockets made of cardboard boxes, broken legged rocking horses gaze the distance with their painted eyes. Colors oozing out from the coloring books. The crystal lens of first love. Maybe this is the time, when I should realize, I was rich all the time. But when you are laying under a gigantic penis, these are just junk. So is money. I would sell the face of my first love just for a sniff of fresh air.

I have no more time to think about this – I notice my hands turning into dark smoke. After a few seconds, my whole body becomes black mist, that flies out from the gigantic penis, out, to the fresh air, leaving the cursed forest far behind.

*

Crawling out from the lamp, my cells begin to cling together again, and I tap myself, hardly believing I have a body. My saviours, the two djinns are just standing there, waiting for me to come to my senses. Then the pervert djinn says: "Look, who's here! The djinn! Tell him your wish!"

The bald, cancerous guy looks at me, with hoping eyes, and he tells me: "I order you, to cure me from cancer!"

The pervert djinn also doesn't hold his wish any longer, opening his coat, showing me his flacid blue prick, with a small wound on it's side, he tells: "I want you, to make this hard again!"

How wonderful. I became a djinn, and now I have to find a cure for cancer and impotence. I will definitely give a bad rating for the seller on the online auction site. Tears spring into my eyes, and I begin to whine like some kind of peevish child: "And what about my wish?"

The two ghosts ask me to follow them. In the place of the next room, there is a giant swimming pool. Our reflections are shaking on the surface of the clean, blue water. I drop to my knees, and begin to drink – swallowing the cool liquid, like crazy. I wash my face, and gulp some more – laughing bubbles into the water. And I couldn't care less, that a dead deer is floating in the middle of the pool.

CUCKOO CUNT

A FLYING BULLET has been chasing the cowboy since he was born. The day he arrived in this world, his father got drunk and shot into the air with his old, measly colt. And the cartridge began its long journey, drilling caverns into the clouds, flying over the yawning deserts, passing around the whole planet, never slowing down, waiting for the moment, to meet the kid, who since became a man, and kill him.

Now and then, it got close enough, so the cowboy could hear it's whooshing sound. At times like this, the man panicked and started to search for a good hiding place – rushing and crouching behind the counter in the saloon, digging himself into the hot sand out in the desert. And once, when he was banging a fat bitch in the whorehouse, he just shrunk in fear, and crawled up into the burly woman. He stayed there for a couple of weeks.

"Oh shit girl, you got knocked up?" the other sluts laughed when they visited the fat bitch in her room, who now couldn't leave her bed because of her heavy distended womb. And when she explained, that she, in fact, is now carrying her former client in her belly, the madam lost her temper, and said: "At least, ask for rent or something! Jesus!"

"Well. I have met a few weirdo's," a prostitute told the fat woman. "There was one, who only got turned on, if I putted a man's clothes on, and he could challenged me with a duel. Imagine us, standing in the rotten sunrise, with hands on our holsters, and I'm about to shit myself, realizing, that he's really going to kill me. But, instead of his gun, he eventually takes out his cock, and starts to fire. Crazy men, I tell ya. The masked bandit didn't want to take off his disguise, not even in bed. I had to suck the barrel of his gun instead of his dick, but he was moaning, like I was playing with the real thing. If you ask me, I think he himself couldn't tell apart which was which anymore. So, I have seen many creeps in this hellhole, but this... This is something new, even for me."

The fat bitch didn't care what the others said; she began to like this client more and more. At nights, she was fondling her round belly, and sang sweet lullabies for him. This made the cowboy fall asleep. One time like this, he was dreaming about his father; he saw him sitting in his old rocking chair, with an empty bottle of whiskey between his yellow fingers, struggling with a hangover.

"Don't be afraid, son, that bullet doesn't chase you anymore," cawed the old man on his rusty voice. "I was out in the yard, when I heard its whooshing sound. So I stood in its way, catching it, closing it into my chest. Here it is now, in this fucking cage, I'll show you!" then he unbuttoned his smudgy shirt, revealing his hollow chest. Buttons lined on that too. He also undid them, and pulled aside his colorless skin, his old meat, showing his ribcage. And there, in the place of his heart, floated a bullet, flying back and forth, like a frightened little canary.

"It can only escape, when I die. Till then, you are safe, son." said the old man, buttoning up his chest.

This dream encouraged the cowboy, so he crawled out from the fat bitch in the morning. The whore couldn't be happier, when she gave birth to him. She wanted to pull the man on to her breasts, but the cowboy refused, got dressed, and walked out of the room, leaving some money on the nightstand.

From that day, he couldn't brush off the fat whore. She was dogging in his footsteps, every time the cowboy was drinking in the saloon, the woman paddled to his table on her pillar-like legs, begging him to come home. The drunken cowboy yelled: "For fuck's sake, leave me alone, you're not my mother!"

This of course made the fat woman cry. She was shouting: "I was the one, who carried you inside my body!"

"Listen to your mama!" laughed the other cowboys from the next table, which made the man's face turn all red. He didn't want this embarrassing scene to go on, so he finished his drink, and went back to the whorehouse on the side of the fat bitch. There, the woman blanketed him, kissing his forehead, singing the same old lullabies that putted the cowboy into a deep sleep again.

In his dream, he saw his father in the same old rocking chair, shaking the empty bottle over his face, trying to get out the last whiskey drips. Then, all of a sudden, he drops the glass and clutches his chest, his face going all violet-colored as he dies. A bloody hole appears on his shirt, as the bullet flies out from its cage.

In the morning, the fat bitch discovers, that her belly is bloated again.

"Gotcha!" She cheers and claps her enormous hands. Then she takes out some yarn and a needle from the nightstand, and sews her hole.

TUMOUR–DJINN

Moaning and snuffling sounds fill the dark in the whorehouse, the sounds of hungry rats. A cuckoo clock hiccups on the wall, distant shootings coming from the streets. In the saloon, people order new skulls – throwing away the old ones, they have drank out the dreams from. The cowboy is roaming in the giant desert in the fat whore's womb. With every step, his feet subside into the warm sand. He listens, looking for the whooshing sound of the bullet, but all he can hear, are the singing cactuses; they echo tune-fragments of old lullabies.

Walking along, he glimpses a small fishing boat between the dunes. Stepping closer, he realizes, that isn't a real boat at all, it's an open coffin, and the sitting fisher in it is his dead father. His skin is all white, the eyes are lightless, and a hole yawns on his chest. The smell of death and alcohol surrounds him; his stiff fingers are holding a fishing rod.

"Dad!" the cowboy greets him. The ghost turns and looks at his son, hissing.

"You're scaring away the fishes!" grumbles the old man. His voice is a rock thrown into a pit. The cowboy looks around in the desert, but he only sees scorpions. They are running next to the coffin on their black needle-like legs. His father pulls out the hook from the sand with a sad look on his face. On the end of the string glints a bullet. The old man adjusts the bait, and throws it back in to the yellow dust.

"Dad." whispers the man, but his father snubs him again. But this time, he adds: "Hurry! You're gonna miss the duel."

"What duel?" The cowboy puckers his brows. The old man points a finger at a distant cactus, and says: "Just stop bothering your old man and go!"

Unbuttoned clouds. Rattlesnakes keep shaking the cuckoo clocks in the end of their tails. Inside them, the sprung birds keep knocking against the wooden walls. They broke. Their small pieces fall out to the sand. They congeal into scorpions; their sprung-tails jumps in the air and poison the sky.

The cowboy is now standing next to the cactus his father had pointed to. Sleepy lullabies come out from the plant.

"Duel." murmurs the man. As he stands and waits there, he notices a creaking noise. From the direction of the town – if there's a town anywhere, the cowboy isn't sure – arrives a woman, pushing a wheelbarrow. The man recognizes the madam of the whorehouse. Her wig is made of dirty rags; her face is like a sleeping shabby cat. In the wheelbarrow lies the bumblebee like fat whore, with a strange smile on her face – like a curved little bone left on the plate.

The cowboy watches the arrivals with emotionless eyes. The creaking of the wheelbarrow's rusty wheel overwhelms the cactuses' sing.

Duel – the word pops into the cowboy's head again, and he places his fingers on to the grip of his gun.

TUMOUR–DJINN

The madam stops thirty feet away; she puts down the wheelbarrow, and walks back to the town. The smile on the fat bitch in the wheelbarrow widens, showing broken board-like teeth. Then she spreads her stumpy legs, revealing the stretching sutures that constrict her vagina lips together.

"Get ready, you bastard, here comes your enemy!" the woman laughs, and the yarn begins to snap. Drops of stream chase each other on the cowboy's forehead.

When the last one, like a long, black eyelash falls out to the sand, the whore starts to scream, her fingers are scratching the side of the wheelbarrow, as the labor pain overwhelms her.

"Get reeeaaady!" she yells, and soon, a bloody little head, like a muskmelon, pops out from her vagina. The cactuses croon; the cowboy watches the scene with an open mouth. The thought that maybe he should help the woman crosses his mind, but his legs aren't moving, his fingers don't let go of the grip.

"This is a duel, and you can't leave your place." a sound in his head reminds him.

It only takes a few minutes, and the baby plops into the sand. As the child squirms, the yellow dust sticks to his wet body like breadcrumbs. A scorpion arrives; it cuts the navel-string, then runs away.

The cowboy takes out his gun, and points it at the sky. His hand trembles.

"No..." he whimpers, trying to stop his own finger, which slowly pulls the trigger. The sharp crack shakes the air – the cactuses swallow their song as the flying bullet wound the clouds. The baby begins to crawl. Dragging himself with his hands and knees. The child is ageing fast. After a few moments, he stands up, and begins to walk woodenly, his hair is growing, and the bones keep lengthening. He looks like a five year old now, but he keeps going and going towards the cowboy. The bullet up in the sky, like an eagle ready to swoop, whizzes back and forth.

The boy is now ten years old. Then eleven. Then twelve. His muscles are wriggling rattlesnakes under the skin. Then vipers. Like black grass, hair grows on his groin. As his features develop, the cowboy recognizes himself in the boy. He drops his gun into the sand, as the bitch in the wheelbarrow screams: "Yeah, that's it, go to daddy, go to daddy!"

Soon, the boy turns into a man, and when he steps to the cowboy, they are almost identical. And the bullet screams.

"No!" moans the cowboy. The cartridge bangs his mirror image in his back.

In the distance, the fisherman yells: "What a catch!"

And death. And hosanna lost in saloon music. The machine erections of scorpions, the clouds like empty doghouses. The cactuses go on fire.

The weeks pass, and the madam gets fed up with the laying bitch. What a no good fat whore, staying all day in bed, the other girls carried food to her room, so she wouldn't starve.

"Stop serving her! This isn't a fucking hotel!" yelled the madam, her eyes rolled so wildly, that they almost fall out of their sockets.

So there were no more breakfasts and dinners in bed. The fat whore's belly rumbled all day long. The whole whorehouse was cracking because of it, and that scared away the clients.

"How could a man cum, when the roof is about to fall on his head?" they grouched, and the dust of the road stole their faces.

There's a pitcher on the nightstand. The fat woman drinks only one gulp every hour. She doesn't want to run out of water. Her unwashed body begins to coalesce with the sheet. She feels the cowboy squirming in her womb. The bitch knows he's starving too.

After a few days, a terrible pain wakes the woman from her sleep, when the carried cowboy begins to bite out pieces from her insides. Just a little, always just a little, from what he finds. She wants to be mad at him, but she can't. Instead, she tries to allure a few rats to the bed, using her sausage-like fingers as bait, hanging them on to the floor. But the rodents don't bite; they just run back and forth under the boards, sometimes moving in the walls, waiting for the woman to die.

She eats out the vulture-feathers from her pillow. On the wall, a cuckoo clock crunches, as it chews the bird inside it. In one morning, the door opens, and the madam steps in.

"So, do you give up, and throw out the guy?" she asks, and the fat bitch, using every effort shakes her head no.

"All right. Then you are both going to die here.," answers the madam. Her nostrils are moving, as she sniffs in the air. "This place stinks." she says with an ugly grimace, stepping to the window, opening it, and then she hurries out of the room. The incoming wind carries street noises – the throbbing of hooves, distant gunshots, laughter, and the clinking of glass. Bear traps clash in the happy hunting ground.

That night, they find the fat bitch dead.

"Was it thirst? Or hunger?" the yawning madam asks the doctor, holding a handkerchief before his face.

"Certainly not." the old doc answers, pulling off the blanket from the big body, revealing a wound on her belly. "This here." he says, scratching his head. "I've never seen anything like it. What a coincidence. The bullet must have flied in the open window, and killed both the mother and her child…"

"That wasn't a fucking child!" yells the madam. And as she drops out these words from her mouth, the clock on the wall begins to chime. But the small wooden doors don't swing open. And the small mechanic bird doesn't jump out. Instead, a metal spring pops out from between the dead woman's legs, tearing apart the black strings. In the end of it hangs a shrunken cowboy corpse. Blood is dripping from his gunshot wound. Then, the spring pulls back the man; he disappears again in the fat woman.

NIPPLES OF A SODA AUTOMAT

A GUY AT the bus station offers a good price for one of my nipples. I finally let him convince me, but I'm eager to know, what does he need it for? He says he keeps an exotic fish at home. The fish only feeds upon human nipples. I inform him that I may consider selling my other nipple too, if he shows me his extraordinary fish. A bit unwillingly he agrees, and we get on the bus together.

The guy lives on the other side of the city, in a timeworn apartment. The door to his flat bristles with locks; it takes most of the morning for him to work a key into each one. By the time we get inside, the rooms of his apartment were bronzed in waning afternoon light.

"You can never be careful enough," he explains, once we're inside, throwing his tennis ball sized key ring onto a table. Stepping into the living room, I notice the big aquarium straightway. In it, a small mermaid girl swims joyfully among the dancing seaweed. The tiny woman's beauty captures me right away – her brown, floating hair, her porcelain skin, the green fan tail, her breasts, which are perfectly formed pearls.

"Wait here!" murmurs the man, heading to the kitchen. I hear him opening the door of the fridge. Then he returns with a plastic box in his hand, full of human nipples. They lay on each other like dead, brown bugs.

"Now watch!" He winks, picking one out, and throwing it into the water. In no time, the small mermaid swims there, catches it, and sitting down on a little treasure tank she begins to chew on the skin.

For a while, we just watch her eat, but then there's a loud knock on the door. The man puts a finger to his mouth. We are listening to the banging for minutes, and then the unknown visitor gives up. Profane words echo through the stairway, then they fade.

"Who was it?" I ask.

He looks distracted and doesn't want to answer my question at first, but then he confesses, that it must have been a former client, who sold his nipples to him.

"They are always coming back! They always change their minds! But what could I do? Somebody has to feed this damn fish! I even cut off my own nipples a long time ago!"

Feeling sorry for the man, I offer to buy his mermaid. He embraces me with tears in his eyes, and brings a pickle jar for the girl. He also gives me the box of nipples, advising me to keep them in the fridge, like mealworms, because at room temperature they can get very mean.

*

I set up a 20 x 11 x 19 inch aquarium, with some seaweed, colorful pebbles, and an oxygen pump that burps bubbles into the water all day. Seemingly, the tiny mermaid is satisfied with her new home, swimming from one corner to another with a wide smile on her face. I just sit and watch her for hours, can't take my eyes off of her. I also can't stop feeding her – though her former owner told me to cater the fish once only a day. But every time I see the mermaid chewing on a nipple, it cheers me up and I began to laugh. She's hilariously cute.

I gaze the mermaid until dawn, then I fall asleep with the half empty box in my lap. And I dream about nipples.

In my dream, I'm wandering in a giant desert, and the thirst is killing me. Yellow wasteland, as far as the eye can see. The heat squeezes the last drops of sweat from my body. Later, I find a soda machine between the dunes. Like a stone, it just stands there in the sand; the sunshine sparks on its hot metal side. Stepping closer, I'm searching my pockets, hoping I have some change somewhere. A sigh of relief escapes my mouth, when I find a few coins, but when I read a sign on the machine, I can't believe my eyes.

The machine doesn't accept money! – It says. Under it, there are buttons and the names of the drinks with the price.

Everything costs one nipple, except the tonic water – that costs two. Thank god, I hate tonic.

Peeking in the automat's window, I see colorful bottles floating in the water, like it was some kind of aquarium. I lick my lips, and decide to sacrifice a nipple. On the side of the machine, hangs a Gillette blade on a chain, available for the help to the customers.

As I cut into my skin with the sharp metal piece, and blood oozes between my fingers, I'm wondering if there's someone stupid, who would cut both of his nipples off just for a tonic.

Strangely I don't feel any pain. I roll the bloody meat between my fingers for a while, then I insert it into the machine's opening. After it's done, I push the cola button. Nothing happens. The machine stays silent. I push another button, but still nothing happens. I press return. Nothing. I start to kick the side of the automat. Then I walk around it, and discover a cardboard sign on it's back: Out of order.

*

Waking up in the afternoon, the tentacles of the dream still straitens my eye. I feel tired, and the mermaid in the aquarium looks pretty bad. Her water is cloudy, like she had diarrhea. Think I've overfed her; she just lays on the oxygen pump, with hands on her stomach. Tiny bubbles stick in her hair.

But there's another problem. The box in my lap is empty – looks like the temperature resuscitated the nipples, they are running up and down in the room on their small insect-leg like hairs, crawling on the walls, disappearing in small cracks. I try to kill them with a newspaper, but they are too fast.

"Nasty little things!" Nods the exterminator guy later, standing in my apartment. He's fat and smells like bacon, his nipples poke out of his sweaty t-shirt. Looking at them, I can't stop thinking about my mermaid. How will I feed her now? Should I start offering money to people for their nipples? Is this true anyway, that she can only eat human nipples?

Looking toward the aquarium, she doesn't look like someone who's thinking about food. Still lying on the pump, her skin is all white, and she pukes small pieces of the nipples into the water – the half digested skin pieces wreathe around her head.

"I'll spray the whole house, that will surely kill them!" explains the guy.

"Is it dangerous stuff?" Should I move out?" I ask, watching a nipple crawling over my wall.

"Nah. Not to people."

After a few minutes, I wander around in a thick smoke cloud. The furniture is like rocks on a misty beach, I try to handhold into them. But I'm getting lost in the cloud, which smells bitter, like tonic.

✶

Like I was walking in a strange new planet, I can't recognize my own apartment anymore. I almost fell over on some furniture hiding behind the smoke. Am I in the kitchen? Or in the living room? I have no idea. I'm yelling to the exterminator guy, but there's no answer. I'm alone. A lonely astronaut on the edge of the galaxy.

Suddenly, something large and massive blocks my way, it's like a closet. But it's illuminated, and as I touch it, it feels more like metal than wood. I realize it's the soda machine. How the hell did this get here?

Its lights shimmer dreamingly – I'm sure it's working now. A digital sign flickers on it's front: PLEASE CHOOSE A PRODUCT.

My fingers are searching for buttons. I find them. Their touch is soft, silky, somewhat like skin. Leaning closer I see that human nipples line up on the machine. I push one of them, and the sound of pleased groaning comes from the automat. But no drink, and the signs don't change either. I try another button. This one's a bit harder and scraggy, but when I push it, the result is the same. The machine just moans lustfully.

Then the idea hits me. Of course, why I didn't think of this. I take my hands away, then bring my face closer to the automat. I take one of the nipples in my mouth, and I begin to suck. Fizzy fluid fills my mouth. Cold and bitter. It's tonic. I hate tonic. I turn my head spitting it out. Wiping my mouth with my shirt, I found two bloodstains on it's front – where it was pressed against my chest.

*

Later, when I come to my senses, the bitter mist still wreathes around me. The automat is gone, only the exterminator guy putters around.

"This stuff… is killing… me…" I whisper to him.

"Yeah, it killed most of the little bastard already!" he cheers, spraying more and more smoke out from his vaporizer. The man is wearing some kind of brown coveralls. When he comes closer, I can see, it is sewn from human nipples. "Just a few days, sir, and you don't have to worry about these little fuckers anymore!"

I want to answer him, but the room is beginning to fade. The waves of the poison wash me away. Later I begin to sink. The cola-cold space freezes my bones.

*

I come to myself after days or weeks. Months maybe? Who knows. The mist is all gone, and I also can't find the exterminator guy. There's just a bill on the table, and a rotting, dead nipple in the bathroom. Apart from that, the house is clean, and all the nipples are gone.

I wash my face and drink some water. Then I take out some moldy cheese from the fridge and bite into it. Tottering into the living room, I gaze at my mermaid. A tiny, half decayed skeleton lies in the stale water, on the oxygen pump. Tiny pearls sit between her rib cage.

THE MARIONETTE MISSIONARY

ROUND AND AROUND– the smell of the jungle, made of used matches – there's a river, with naked reptiles in it. Somewhere, an old negro lady is carving coffins from the trees. Then she carves out a few dead too, so they could hold a blessed funeral. From her back, a lying missionary encourages her, "Yes, yes, you're doing it right! Now this is gonna be a real Christian burial, everybody should come and see in this damned, paganish jungle. No more cannibalism, no more necrophilia, these things must stay in the closet!"

So the woman keeps carving out the coffins and the dead, but she avoids one tree that has hungry piranhas as leaves. If a monkey crawls up, the tree devours its flesh, and a skeleton made of black matchesfalls onto the wet ground.

"Stop dodging that tree!" orders the missionary. "Our Lord cherishes pain and mortification!" (He says, but really, he reads this like his soul was touching the braille words of Christ's wounds.)

A rain arrives – the tears of ancient gods washes the round bellies of pregnant negro woman. Then the rainbows break and the colors die – the world drowns into blackness. The Moon crawls up to the sky, and snarls at the stars, these shining predator eyes. A giant leech hangs on its round pale belly, sucking out the light from its celestial body. Then a new morning rises, here in the jungle, where killer orchids open their petals, and chew on hummingbirds. A giant crocodile bites an oar into half, slurping out the marrow. The minute hands fall out from the old clocks and turn into blood sucking worms.

"Ka–ta–klak!" the alligator-people yell, sitting on the river shore, masturbating, fantasizing about native woman, with acidulous vaginal fluids that even dissolve the exoskeletons of bugs. The door of a forgotten dream knocks on their ugly skulls – the never ending dark nightmare of running waters – broken flutes play music inside their hearts – the sooty ghost of time spins and spins – a fish with razorblade-scales dances in the night of their pupils.

"Ta–klaaak!" the reptile-people moan. The sunlight glimmers on their flying green sperm, and their faces are now broken plates.

A few miles away, the missionary is now standing in the cloudy water, baptizingnative hunters. The priest is sizingthe negro men on the shore.

"What a dirty little gathering!" he mumbles under his nose. The warriors are all naked, their eyes are empty bird nests. Long, black penises hang down on to their knees, bone-rings tinkle in their foreskin.

"All right, let's get over with this." sighs the holy man, and he waves for the first to step into the water. The missionary grimaces in disgust, when he sees that the bloody scalp of an infant hanging out from his mouth.

"My God, what am I doing here among these people?" growls the priest, then he reaches out his hand, like a rigorous teacher who just caught his student chewing gum. The warrior spits the bloody skin into his palm, along with a great amount of pink saliva.

"The true children of Christ doesn't eat human! How many times do I have to tell you?" he yells, throwing the shred into the water. A fish arrives, it swallows it then swims away.

"Now let's start, or we'll never finish!" says the missionary, putting his hands on the dark fellow's wide shoulder.

"I baptizeyou in the name of the Father Son and Holy… shit, why won't you sink?" The priest tries to force the mighty man down, but he just stands there, still like a stone statue, looking at him with motionless white eyes.

"Just squat, you idiot!" The missionary shows him what to do. Finally, the black hunter gets the idea and repeats his moves. But when he sinks and the grey waves crash over his head, the warrior turns into a giant catfish, and slips out from the proselytizer's hands.

"What the fuck?" The white man curses. "Well, okay, this one's gone for sure. May the devil take his soul. Who's next?"

And a new negro arrives. But when he descends, he too turns into a giant catfish and swims away. The forenoon takes down it's skin. Monkeys scream among the trees. The natives arrive one by one – stepping into the water, but every time their heads disappearunder the water, they turn into fishes and vanish in the depths. The missionary can't take it any longer, and he crawls out of the river, murmuring, "To Hell with you all then! Pagans! Go back to your ugly statues, your bloody rituals then, what do I care? But you're all gonna cry when the flames of Hell are kissing your asses!"

On the shore, he discovers tiny black leeches hanging on his hairy legs.

"Oh! That puts the lid on it!" he sighs, beginning to strike off the worms with his Holy Bible. No use. Then he drops some holy water on the animals, which makes them fall into the grey mud. He kicks back the leeches into the river. A big splashing starts in the water as the giant catfishes fight over the worms. Gaping, round mouths rise to the surface.

"So you're back?" The missionary gets all red, and he throws the first thing at them he can find. The Holy Bible falls into the river with a big splash, and the water starts to boil, as the fishes strike at the prey.

"The sacred words! What have I done?" The priest immediatelyjumps after the book. "Dear Christ, I'll save you! You've suffered enough already!"

The hungry, wild fish spring at the man. They bite away the missionary's marionette strings that were moving him from the clouds. The puppet-priest floats while the fish keep pecking him, then the animals get bored of the wooden man, and they head into the depths to find some other prey. The drift carries away the helpless Marionette

The jungle cries. A giant snake swallows down a coat hanger. A black comb, like a centipede crawls away on a giant fleshy leaf. Down by the river, a negro woman stands in the cool water, washing out the blood and the splinters from her tired hands. Then a big piece of wet wood knocks her on the legs. She looks down. It's a wooden puppet. She carries it out to the river shore, and lays the Marionette into a carved out coffin.

The sun falls, hitting a monkey in the head. Some warriors arrive, poking their fingers into the animal's open skull, they paint tribal signs on their face with the blood. One of them draws a cross on his cheek, then disappearsbetween the trees, and the death-screams of animals fill the forest.

The night sticks out its forked tongue. Sick catfishes are squirming in the mud. Their stomachs are full of indigestiblebook pages. They are dying, pukingtheir unholy souls at the sky.

SECRET SKULL HOUSE

SOME BRATTY BOYS from the neighborhood decide to make a secret clubhouse in my skull. They don't ask me about it, but I have no argument against the plan. So, every afternoon getting home from school they occupy my head. The kids laugh loudly, and crack their chip bags. Sometimes smoke flies out of my ear. I suspect they are experimenting with their first cigarettes. Of course, I was just like them when I was their age, so I'm not going to tell on them; that's for sure. If only they wouldn't leave such a mess every time. It can be really awkward, when having a conversation with someone I begin to shake or nod my head and suddenly a crumpled porn magazine falls out from my ear.

Soon, the parents get wind of the secret clubhouse, and they step into my apartment swinging a bone saw. They insist on looking in my skull; telling me they have the right to know what their boys are up to behind their backs.

Now, the kids and I are both punished – they are grounded in their rooms, as for me, the parents won't give back my skullcap. It's quite embarrassing. Going to work in the mornings some cheeky brats on the bus are having a great time pushing spitballs and chewed bubble gum between my brain wrinkles when I'm not looking.

That's enough, I decide one morning, I have rights too. So I knock on the mother's door, who has my upper head.

She just stands there in the door, smoking, holding my skullcap in her hand, which looks like a half hairy coconut, and she flicks the ash into it. After I'm done with my speech about human rights, she slams the door in my face.

I have no time for a second round I must leave to work. Scratching out a used ticket from my brain wrinkles I catch the next bus. A young couple whispers and chuckles behind me. I quickly get off at the next stop, before they could plan a secret date in my occipital lobe.

THE KIDNEY STONE INFANT

SPASMODIC PAIN TORTURES me, and my urine seems bloody. I suspect I have kidney stones, so I visit the doctor. The ultrasound test shows a clay-pigeon growing inside me. The doc writes me a prescription for antiepileptic drugs and for some tap water, telling me, that this will help my body to get rid of the rock. Finally, he makes a call for the local rifle club, just to be sure, a gunman will always be around me. I ask if they could remove the clay-pigeon by surgery, but the doctor shakes his head, "Well, you know, the hospital is running out of money, so we don't do surgeries anymore. We only take action if it's really necessary, otherwise, the scalpel stays in the cabinet." he mumbles. His pupils are dissolving pills. Then he pats my shoulder, saying,"Be a man and give birth to it!"

So a guy wearing an ear defender is always on my back, following me everywhere, and when I need to piss, he stands behind me, cocking his gun. And every time I put my dick back in to the pants, he lowers the weapon with a disappointed face.

"Sorry." I tell him, but it seems these false alarms make him more and more angry. His eyes glint at me like barb wire. At night, I watch him standing beside my bed, pointing the riffle at my crotch, his sweaty fingers are dancing on the trigger. He doesn't let me turn off the lights, telling me he would miss the target in the dark, and I'm starting to fear that eventually his hands will grow tired, and he will shoot me right in the balls while I sleep. So I take a few pills, and that knocks me out, therefore I don't have to think about that riffle anymore.

In the morning, I wake up in the middle of a green field. I'm layingon an operating-table, the doc stands beside me. He pulls aside his surgical mask, telling me, "I'm sorry, it looks like you're not a man enough to give birth to this pigeon. We must do the surgery."

I sneak a look behind me. There stands the whole rifle club, with guns on their shoulders. Birds fly over the sky. It's a beautiful summer day; a fat bee buzzes in front of my face, then it descends onto my chest, rubbing its tiny black legs like a cartoon villain making up an evil plan. Looking at it closer, I realize it's a painkiller pill, only with wings and tiny legs. I try to catch and swallow the pilule-bug, but it flies away. What a beautiful summer day! Gauze strips are hissing under the rocks, birds with medical scissor-heads are picking tiny squirming catheter tubes out from the ground, loose radiograph-kites disappear among the clouds. The scalpel between the doc's fingers shine, and when he cuts me open, I realize he forgot to anesthetize me. Maybe the hospital doesn't have any money for that. I don't really mind, I'm still doped by the painkillers, my bored gaze just elbows out on my eyelids, and I'm watching as the doc's hands disappearin the hole inside me. I'm biting the air every timea painkiller-bee fliesby. My blood is dripping on to the grass. The doctor soon pulls out something dark and round. He cheers, and throws it up in the air. The gunmen fire behind me, like angry bulls, rifle butts run against the bony shoulders, and the whole field shakes from the explosions. Something falls into the ground, smoking. The doc walks to it, picking it up he looks over the hole that a bullet left in the strange object.

"Sorry, it was one of your kidneys!" he apologizes, then he returns, plugging his hand back inside me. Next, he routs out my spleen, but I have no time to warn him, it too flies into the air and the rifle club fires.

Again the doc asks for my pardon, and soon, my liver passes across the sky. It continues like this for a while, then after an hour, he finallycomes across the clay-pigeon, and the riflemen destroy it. It explodes, and the splinters wound the birds. I thank the doc, who looks at his watch, and runs away, leaving his bloody gloves behind. I stagger to my feet from the operating-table and I start to collect my holey organs, packing them back inside my body with shaking hands, trying to figure out which goes where, but really, I have no clue. They fall out again. I look at the members of the rifle club, but the men just lay there, smoking cigarettes and drinking beer.

"Could you give me a hand?" I ask them.

They stare at me and my organs. One of them shrugs, and brings me the nylon bag, still cold from the beers.

"Thanks." I growl, putting my insides into the bag. I decide to reassemble myself at home, with the help of anatomy pictures on the net. Who knows why, I pick up the doc's messy gloves too, and wave goodbye to the riflemen with them.

*

A strange scene greets me at home. Stepping into my bedroom I find myself between the sweaty sheets, I'm screaming in pain, pointing at my crotch. I throw away the bloody bag, and run to myself. I look like someone who's going to give birth: my pisshole widens like a gaping mouth, something is pushing itself through my urethra. Grabbing my hands, I tell myself that I can do it, I just have to push harder. Seemingly, I don't believeany of my words, I just curse myself, but knowing that only the pain makes me say these things, I forgive myself. Looking for some painkillers, I realize that I already took all of them. The pill bottle is full of fallen-out bee stingers and filmy wings.

"Doesn't matter! We'll do this anyhow!" I encourage myself, and we are doing it: my penis is so fat now, like an anaconda digesting an antelope, and soon, it pukes out a round clay-pigeon. But then, I realize that the ceramicobject ends in a neck. The neck ends in shoulders and a tiny chest. It's a baby. A real child is coming out. I couldn't imagine a penis giving birth to an infant, but it's happening now in frontof my eyes. My dick is a bursting hose pipe. In no time, the premature looking little man falls into my hands. As he wiggles with his stumpy arms and legs, he sprays bloody mucus into my face. The child, apart from having a clay-pigeon instead of a head, and the fact that he was born from a penis and not a vagina, looks completely healthy and normal. A long, tremulous umbilical cord connects the crying infant with my run-down cockhead. I watch me standing before myself, holding the child, with tears of joy gathering in my eyes.

"Say hello to daddy!" I stick the infant into my face, and I know we're gonna raise the kid together. Me and me and the child, we're gonna be a beautiful family. Of course, there will be people talking behind our backs, pointing at us with their severe fingers, mocking the poor boy, because he has a clay-pigeon for head and he was delivered by a man; but right now, I really don't care. It's is the happiest moment of my life.

And this is when the rifleman steps into the room. The one who was following me in the last couple of days. He must have been in the toilet, or hiding somewhere in the house. A surprise comes to his sandpaper face, when he glimpses at the kid.

"There flies the bird!" he yells, raising the gun to his shoulders. And he fires. The infant's clay head explodes, and sharp splinters wound up the wallpaper.

THE VIOLIN–FISHERS

SHADOWS OF CIRCLING seagulls stick to the heated rocks on the bay. Sleepy seashells blink at naked boyswho drag their fishnets to the shore. Their spines chamber out from their backslike snakes hiding under the sand. The rope bites into their sunburnt shoulders. In the unfolding net, along with silver fish and purple crabs, a dozen violins squirm. Their strings are covered with seaweed and flutter in excitement, gills discharging on their brown sides, pushing out the remaining salty water from their bodies. One of the older boys sticks two fingers into a gill, stretching it open, and shows it to his little brother.

"Look! It's just like a pussy!" He winks at the kid, and the other boys start to laugh. Seagulls swoop down to the sand, eye the fish in the net, but suddenly the sharp sound of a horn scares the birds away. The fisherboys look back at the road where an old truck is parked, a fat, hairy hand hanging out the front window, waving for them to hurry up. So the boys pick up the violins, and run to the truck—they throw the musical instruments into the hot metal truck bed, where they keep squirming and jumping. When they rub their bodies together, their strings squeak.

A fat man leans out of the van. Sweat glistens on his round face, the hairs of his tiny mustache collect the salty drops. His stained yellow undershirt is like a map leading to nowhere—and the ashes of his burning cigar keep falling on it. The boys finish with the packing. The oldest one runs to the driver, who fishes out some greasy money from the glove compartment and slaps it into the kid's palm. He nods and turns the key. The engine roars and the truck disappears over the horizon. The boys runs back to the shore, where one of the nets still wobbles with a violin inside.

"Okay, let's build a fire!" orders the biggest boy, and the other children scatter along the beach.

"Tonight's program: Debussy" says a poster in front of the opera house. A truck drives into the parking lot, and when the driverhonks the horn, musicians in suits arrive, pick up the dried violins, and walk back into the building.

The driver steps out of the truck, stretching and cracking his joints. Feeling a bit dizzy from the heat, he staggers through the stage door. In his dressing room, he pulls off his sweaty undershirt, throws it in the corner, then opens a closet and takes out an elegant suit. He stubs his cigar in the ashtray and gels his hair back.Someone knocks on his door.

"Are you ready, maestro?"

And the maestro is ready. There's an aquarium next to the mirror with a giant sea urchin inside. Dipping his hand into the water, he pulls out one of its spines.

In the concert hall the musicians are tuning their new instruments—some of them are blowing huge sea shells, others are touching the jellyfish tentacles of a harp. As bows touch strings, the violins come to life—their gills begin to purge, puking salty water onto the musician's shoulders. The audience rumbles as obese women in their choking tight cocktail dresses, pearls clinking against each other on their huge necks, turn to their yawning husbands and poke them with sausage fingers. When the maestro walks to his podium, the sound of clapping rises. The man bows, thenraps the music stand with his baton.

In the meantime, flames rise on the shore, and the fire begins to chew on some broken oars. The oldest boy is skinning the violin with a knife. The blood of the instrument drips into the sand. He cuts out the inedible parts, and throws the gills at the tiny boy next to the fire.

"Here ya go, marry it!" he mocks the boy. "This is the only pussy you're ever gonna get!"

The other boys begin to laugh, while tears well up in the corners of the child's eyes. He jumps up and runs into the night.

The laughter chases him for a while, then meshes with the roar of the sea's dark waves.

As the maestro warms up, he sweats, as if he were still sitting in the truck. The waves of music run at the rocks wrapped in cocktail dresses and blow into spray of notes. The musical keys turn the husbands on and they grow young again—turning into bronzed boys.As they laugh, their penises grow hard and ejaculate. White pearls roll out of their trousers, and their wives begin to chase the small spheres, trampling each other, eventually becoming entangled in the boy-nests. The little fishermen sharp each musical note they find in the air.

"Okay, let's build a fire!" orders the biggest boy, and they huddle their seats up. The shells on their chests begin to clap. The wailing of fat ladies drowns out the sound of the instruments. The maestro perceives the muddle, but he simply can't stop conducting, not even when the boys carry away his podium and throw it on the fire. His baton smolders like a cigar, but it doesn't stop at his fingers: soon his whole arm turns to ashes and drops to the ground.

The boys watch the fire bite into the meat—the cosmic notes of stars on the mirror of the sea—under the light of the moon the violins swim in the bay, casting a greenish light under the waves, laying their eggs in the sludge.

On the other side of the bay, the young boy sits crying on a rock, watching the distant glow of the instruments. Then he notices something, on the shore, in the cool sand, a giant dark mound stirs. The boy stands and sneaks up on it. It's a beached piano—digging into the sand with its slim legs. The child watches its wide, gleaming dark side in amazement—its giant gills open and close continuously, foamy water oozing out on the sand. The boy extends his tiny hand and touches one of its keys. The instrument shakes in fear, its legs dig deeper pits into the sand, as it tries to drag itself back into the water. And then the boy smiles. He sticks two fingers into its enormous gill, stretching it open.

*

Colorful tourists arrive—their skins are gleaming with sunscreen—and take pictures of the beached whale. Photoflashes sparkle.

"Poor, poor thing," the parents say, while their children throw sand in the animal's small, black eyes. They argue and crawl back into their cars, turning the keys and then disappearing down the roads, while whale screams come out of their cameras.

Dusk oozes from the sky's wounds. A wind arrives from the sea, dancing a poster onto the shore. As it sticks to the heated rocks, the sign comes legible. Tonight's program: Debussy. Then the hot stone sets the paper on fire and it turns to ashes.

The audience arrives. They gather around the whale in dinner jackets and cocktail dresses. The giant mammal is almost dead— an assembly of ghosts stirs in its fading dark eye. The recently arrived take their seats in the sand, waiting for Debussy—

scraping the wax out of their ears, kneading tiny pearls. They hold their breath, and throw the ones whose hearts are beating too loudly into the water. Then the mouth of the whale opens; musicians tune their instruments in the animal's giant throat-hall. What beautiful acoustics! A lady in the audience pisses herself upon hearing these semitones. A podium stands on the whale's tongue. Shells of hands clap when the maestro arrives. The baton goes erect in his hand, and finally the show begins; music fills the shore—levitating above the waves—in distant hotels, cameras in bags begin to cry.

But then, something interrupts the program. The sound of laughter and whoops, naked boys running between the rocks, yelling, shouting, their penises lashing against their bare thighs. Knives glitter in their hands.

The maestro grunts angrily, and he signals to the musicians to play more loudly. But the waves of music can't wash away the rampage of the boys. The maestro can't bear it any longer, and he shouts; "You're ruining the performance, you rats! This is Debussy!" He shakes with anger, but the boys just keep laughing at him. The audience feels ill at ease, a few ladies die silently in embarrassment, the others, when they notice the sharp little knives in the boys' hands, jump up and run away. The kids don't care about them, they are mocking the maestro, shouting; "Yoouu're ruinining the perfomance, this iiiis Debuuusy!" One of the boys gets an erectionand begins to sway his cock back and forth, as if he's conducting the music. As he rolls his hips the musicians get confused and the music slides into chaos. The maestro hits the podium with his baton and it breaks in two. Then he aims at the boys with his wand, ready to throw it like a dart. (The spines of the sea urchin are poisonous, causing temporary paralysis. The time before the poison takes effect is about the same as the lengthof Debussy's La Mer.) He almost throws it, when the whale suddenly closes its mouth. The boys can hear as the maestro begins to curse inside the mammal, locked in a music-storm. They give the animal a clap, and one of them shouts: "Come on boys, let's push it back into the water!"

So they gather around the dying whale, and start to put their shoulders into the behemoth. The boys' muscles ache, the animal leaves a deep gash in the sand as it gets closer and closer to the sea. The withdrawing waves are helping the kids, and soon the animal's body spins into the foam. The boys are waving goodbyes to the whale as it sprays mist into the dark sky. All of a sudden something blocks its blowhole. It's the maestro, he got caught in there, shouting curses, then the animal blows again, and like a champagne cork he flies into the night sky: "Forgive me, Debuussyyyy!"And he disappears into the depths.

*

Morning arrives, all the boys on the beach open their eyes at once. They stand, stretching as small crayfish fall from their chests. Their morning wood points at the sea, while they kick away the black remains of yesterday's fire. Suddenly, they hear music. It's coming from the other side of the bay. The boys grab their knives and begin to run.

After a few moments, they glimpse the broken-legged piano and the little boy. His tiny fingers are moving on the keys. Sweat is running down his forehead, and his face shines as he plays. The fisherboys give each other a flustered look. The little pianist smiles at his brothers victoriously. They must be very proud of him now. His fingers keep running over the keys, like the needle legs of a crayfish in the sand. As if he weren't controlling his own hands, as if the music were simply nesting itself under his nails.

But then, the oldest boy yells, his voice a knife thrust into the piano-piece: "Meat!"And the other boys don't need any more encouragement: they charge at the instrument and begin to chop it all up, slicing hunks of meat from the piano. The little boy is horrified. He wants to scream and run away, but his legs don't move. He just keeps his fingers on the keys, and he plays and plays, while his brothers throw the meat into bloody mounds, and the instrument slowly disappears beneath his fingers.

CROTCH-COUCH

IT IS DAMN sure that this was the last time I let myself get talked into any furniture buying. Okay, we do need a couch, and it only took us one day to decide that leatherette is out of the question because it is not really durable. Fabric is too average. So we chose leather. The size wasn't a question. We just measured the wall that it will stand against. But picking the color is harder than I would imagine. Right now, my wife is vacillating between jazzberry jam purple and purple pizzazz, but every unknown shade of purple and red came into question already. She talks only about colors for three weeks or so. We didn't make love for almost two weeks. And last week, she tried to tear down the dress from a little girl in the bus, yelling, "This is the color! This is it!"

While the policemen were questioning her, she just cried, and mumbled "I'm so sorry, I made a mistake. It's not that color at all. Looking at it in the sunlight, this red seems terrible; it would ruin our living room for sure."

Instead of going to the movies, having dinner in a restaurant or simply just taking a walk, we go to furniture stores, and I start to believe, that the color my wife is searching for really doesn't exist.

"Please, just one more, just one more store!" she begs, so we step into another one, where a drunk looking man with a greasy mustache stares at us with red eyes. A sign in the shop window assured us that here we will find every possibly shade, so my woman launches into her usual speech about cochineal insects that dry a little brownish under the sweltering sun. The man puckers his eyebrows, then he shouts for his wife. A thin, miserable looking woman staggers out from the office. She could be a poster model for Amnesty International, old punch marks cover her face, nowhere leading maps of healing scars. The shop keeper orders her, "Undress, bitch!", and when she takes off her blouse, a dozen fresh scars come into sight around her bra strap – red, purple and blue ones. My wife leans closer concentrating on the newer marks, finally pocking at one and saying "This is almost good. But it's not vivid enough."

The shop keeper nods, and then asks for our patience. He locks himself into the office with his wife. The sounds of yelling and smacks emanate from behind the door. I look at my wrist watch and sigh. When they finally return, the crying woman's face is all red.

"This… This is just horrible!" my wife mutters. "It should be a bit lighter."

The mustached man soon gives up, and leaving the store we go home. Lost in our thoughts we walk the streets hand in hand, but really, it feels like I'm holding a stranger's palm. An imaginary couch is standing between us. At home, my wife tells me "Awful, did you notice how pushy and violent that seller was?" she complains. "He almost talked us into a cheap poppy color!"

*

Not having any chance for sex again, I decide to search for some porn on the net. I'm sick of couches and colors, and my dick is so hard I could knock out the wall with it. My saliva is dripping as I watch a teenaged girl working a rolling pin sized vibrator up her tight pussy on the monitor. I'm almost there, when I hear a scream coming from behind my back, "Good Lord!"

It's my wife. I try to cover the screen with my smeary fingers, but she rushes over, pushing my hand aside, and the young girl comes into view. All of a sudden, I would give anything if the girl wouldn't be naked, wishing if she were at a cafe bar, writing her homework, but of course she's still nude and the dildo still hangs out of her. I'm making up lies in my head, for example, saying that this is just a French art movie, and nowdays all the european films are full of scenes like this, but when I try to explain myself, she interrupts, yelling "This is it!"

I gaze at her confused, asking, "What you mean?"

"The color I was looking for!" She points at the young girl's vagina. "Don't you see?"

"I see, I see…" I mummble staring away. Looking at another woman's pussy in the company of my wife is quite embarrassing. "Are you… uh… sure?"

"Move aside!" She pushes me away from the computer, clicking on new and new porn videos, licking her lips while staring at the vaginas of the freshly appearing net-whores. I begin to suspect that this whole color thing is just an excuse, and she's turned on somehow by these videos, which will possibly lead to a great fuck session. So I feel rather disappointed when she closes the new pages, and gets back to the paused video of the first seen teenaged girl, saying "I'm sure. This is the one." And tears begin to form in her eye. She falls into my neck. "It will look gorgeous in the living room!" She saves a still image from the video to the desktop, and clicks on print. Soon, the machine spits out a page with the young girl petrified in ecstasy. She hands me the picture: "Be so nice and take this to the department tomorrow. Tell them this is what we want!"

I think she must be joking. Or that this is some kind of childish revenge for catching me watching an adult movie.

"I'm not going to show pictures of genitals in the store!" I growl, but looking at her, seeing her angry eyes, I already know that yeah, that's exactly what I'm going to do tomorrow.

*

Wringing my hands in embarrassment I step into the department store. A spectacled young seller comes to me – he recognizes me straightaway, we've been here at least three times with my wife last week. The porn pic is in my pocket, I smile at him oddly, considering running out of the shop, but of course that wouldn't solve anything – the mad color search, the whole crazy situation at home would continue, this way at least I can put an end to it. So I ask the guy if we could talk somewhere in private. He stares at me suspiciously for a few moments, then he shrugs and takes me to a small office. There I slide the paper into his hands, and I almost die in shame when he unfolds it. The sellers professionalism surprises me. After studying the photo for a while, he smiles and nods, telling me it's soluble and the production time is two weeks. I almost jump for joy, and return home with a big smile on my face.

Some wonderful days come – we don't talk about the couch anymore, we throw out the home decor magazines, and we make love every night. Now and then I catch my wife looking at the calendar where she circled the day of the delivery, but I don't say anything, just smile at her.

But the idyll soon comes to an end, when on the circled day some workers arrive, carrying a gigantic human vagina into our living room.

*

We stand side by side, looking at the enormous pussy laying on our carpet. It only takes a few minutes for my wife to burst into tears.

"This... This isn't what I wanted at all!" she cries, and I don't know what to answer. Finally I tell her, "Well, I... I kinda like it."

As it lies on its side, our new furniture could be easily mistaken for the lips of a woman, but of course we both know exactly what it is. A strange, but somehow familiar odor fills the room. I step closer, and poke the pink flesh with my finger.

"It matches with the wall." I mumble, but when the thing begins to leak transparent fluid on to the carpet, my wife screams, "Take it back! Replace it! Buy a new one!"

"Oh no I don't!" I shout angrily. "Do you know how much it cost? And I'm not just talking about money! I'm sick to death!"

"It can't stay here!" she yells back.

"I… I kinda like it." I tell her, and of course this is just oil to the flames. She assures me that it's all my fault, that I fucked up the order.

"Oh really? Why didn't you go to the store then, and stick that porn pic up to the seller's nose yourself?" She then tells me that I'm useless, and a disgusting pervert. After making that clear, she runs in to the bedroom, returning she throws a pillow at me, saying, "If you like that couch so much, sleep on it!"

She then slams the door. I sigh. Sitting down to our new furniture, I burry my face into my palms. I wonder why we needed a new couch anyway. Later, I begin to curse the sky when I notice that the mysterious liquid oozing out from our new furniture has totally soaked my trousers.

TUMOUR–DJINN

*

Darkness surrounds me. The sounds of stifled crying and soft whimpers coming from the bedroom keeps me awake. I'm listen to it for a while, then I try to cover my ears. After some time, silence broods over the house. Only the ticking of a clock tears the spider web of my thoughts. I'm lying naked on our new couch. My soaked pyjamas are drying somewhere in the corner. As minutes go by, a strange calmness descends on me. Of course I only chose the new furniture just to show my wife that I do like it. But now, I really begin to like it – it's comfy, it's smooth, it's warm. And yes, wet too, but that doesn't bother me anymore. Long forgotten feelings carry me away – I feel safe, like I was in my mother's womb again. The hot pussy lips lean on me like flower petals, which gives a feeling that I'm sinking. I squirm a bit, just to find the perfect position, every time I move, the whole couch begins to shake in pleasure, its lips become more wet and warm, sucking my body deeper. That familiar sweet smell fills my lungs, and I become erect. The sparks of joy crackle behind my eyes, as the pussy moves under me, sliding me back and forth, like I was a forming pearl in a seashell in the bottom of the ocean. Sometimes traveling to the edge of the furniture I almost fall down to the ground, but then, that sucking power again swallows me back to the depths of the couch. The massage is effective; my body shudders as I cum. Then all the movement stops. Laying, curling up in fetus pose, the waves of a dream drifts me away, and my final thought is that I really, really pleased with our new couch.

*

Waking up with a smile on my face and looking all relaxed just makes my wife angry again. She throws a glass into the dishwasher. Sharp splinters fly everywhere.

"You stink!" she screams running out of the kitchen. Looks like I have to sleep on the couch again tonight. And I really don't mind.

*

A few days pass, and I notice a terrible scream coming from the living room. It's my wife, her face is all white and she's pointing at the couch, yelling, "It's… It's menstruating!"

Indeed, blood oozes out from the vagina, I rush over and quickly roll up the carpet. Bringing a floor cloth I begin to clean up the mess, while my wife can't stop screaming into my ear: "It's bleeding, it's bleeding!"

"Yeah, well, sometimes they do, I don't think I have to explain it to you!" I growl, still cleaning the floor. So much blood. Like if the room turned into some kind of crime scene.

"Throw out that fucking ugly thing!" My wife beats the wall with her fists.

"Don't worry, it will stop soon." I don't know who I'm calming – my wife or the sofa.

TUMOUR–DJINN

"I don't care! I don't want it here!" she cries, and rushes out of the room. I hear the slamming of the front door, and peeping out in the window, I watch her walking through the street, sweeping tears from her face. I'm sure she's heading to her mom. She usually goes to her when we're having a fight. To tell her what a big prick I am. Never mind, she'll calm down eventually. Till then, I've got work to do. I collect some old clothes, mostly raunchy t-shirts and smudgy socks, and I tuck them into the crack of the couch. Later, I decide to rope some of these clothes and form a giant tampon.

Tapping the side of the giant pussy I realize, that I can't sleep on the couch tonight. And I'm still an unwelcomed guest in my own bedroom. So I make my bed on the floor, near to the bleeding vagina.

*

Weeks go by, and we live like total strangers together with my wife – just wandering around around each other, sometimes crossing eachother's field of vision. I really don't know why she must make such a big deal about a couch, and sure, I would throw out the damned furniture, just for the sake of peace, if I could forget about that one month madness that preceded the buying.

She's just getting what she earned, I remind myself, and I shlep to the couch to sleep. A crazy dream haunts me. In my dream I take my wife to a restaurant, and when I pull the chair out from beneath the table for her, I discover that it has a giant, brown wooden penis – it throbs and honey like resin is leaking from it. I insist my wife to sit into another chair, but when I pull out another one, it too has a dick – maybe even bigger, than the first one. My wife gets unpatient and sits down on the first chair – I make a grimace when she moans and smiles, telling me, that I should put my butt down, so we can order.

"I'm… I'm not gonna sit on that… thing!" I growl, and I ask the waiter to bring me a new chair. He brings one. And it too has a prick.

"What the fuck? What kind of place is this? Jesus, I'll just stand then." I yell, and when I look at my wife I become jealous. "And you! Stop rocking on that chair! And wipe off that stupid grin from your face!"

I wake up. The dream leaves a strange feeling of guilt in me. I totter into the kitchen, to drink a glass of water. When I turn the lamp on, I find a small note on the table. My wife wrote it. She moved to her mother for a week. "Don't come after me. I'll come back, and we'll talk about the couch."

Going back to the living room, I feel a strong desire to spend the night in our bedroom, in our good old bed. But then I realize that I'm all messy, vaginal fluid covers me and I would just mess up the sheets. So I lay back to my place, to the couch. It wiggles under me like a waterbed, trying to massage me, but I'm not in the mood for any games now. When I fall asleep again, I dream about the pussy-couch. It strangles me with slimy squid like tentacles.

*

Waking up with a bad back ache. Something is pressing against my side. There's a tiny bulge in the pussy-couch. I roll over. The morning sun shines into my face. (One of the disadvantages of the living room.) I wonder about that bulge. Something must have gotten nipped under the pink skin-wrinkles. Some keys or a purse maybe. Sitting up I feel it up with my fingers. Then I push aside the labia, sneaking under the skin my mouth drops open. I find a tiny developing embryo that strangely reminds me of a featherless chicken. I begin to sweat. How will I explain this to my wife? Seemingly I knocked up our sofa.

Walking up and down in the house, I'm trying to find a solution. Maybe I should hire some workers who would carry the furniture into a hospital, and get an abortion. But I couldn't bear the shame, the look in to the doc's face; he would immediately realize I had sex with a piece furniture. He would sure send me to the nuthouse. Maybe I should try to perform the abortion myself, but the idea makes me throw up. Besides, I have always been an anti-abortionist – though I have never gotten anyone pregnant before, especially not a couch.

The best solution would be – maybe – to fish out the fetus from the couch somehow. If I could stick it up to my wife when she sleeps, she would believe it is our child. But I'm afraid it would be more than suspicious after not having much sex with her lately.

Eventually, I do nothing. And a week passes by. And I stop sleeping on the couch.

*

After who knows how many days, the door opens, and my wife steps into the house. It's like she's changed somehow, she looks all relaxed, that old light smolders in her eye. I'm standing in the living room with an embarrassed look on my face, like a young boy who's been caught doing something naughty, standing, trying to cover the bulge on the couch with my body, though I don't think my wife would notice it anyhow, it's still so little.

"We need to talk…" I stutter under my nose, but my wife gives me a flirty smile, telling me, "Later, babe, later." Then she kisses me. Passionately, like we were teenagers again. I'm sure that her mother's hand is in this. I assume she recommended this tactic to my wife, she always says that there's only one way to control a man. Well, I would be a fool to tell my wife that she was right all the time, and yes, the couch must go. That would spoil the fun for sure.

"Did you miss me, big boy?" she purrs, pushing me playfully on to the couch. The giant pussy squelches as my wife crawls on too, with only slight disgust on her face, that fades away fast. I'm sure we are going to have sex here for a purpose, so she can tell me later, that yes, she tried out the new furniture, just to please me, and nope, she didn't like it at all.

"Yeah, I really missed you." I admit, while her fingers unbutton my shirt.

"Very good!" She winks at me, and we get out of our clothes. Like wet snails stuck together, we roll on the wet pussy-couch. When I get over her, I'm hard as a rock, ready to penetrate her, but then, she hisses painfully.

"Ouch!" She moves away. "There's something under me."

The blood runs out of my face. Also, it runs out of my penis too, which starts to soften. My wife discovers the bulge under her. And before I could say anything, she begins to beat it with her fists. I can hear a quiet cracking sound, I can almost see, how the developing little bones crack into pieces under the pink skin.

"There. That's better." She says, spreading her legs. "Now come, you devil!"

I swallow and close my eye. Using every effort I get hard again. As I slide into her, and our bodies begin to wave, I burry my face to her neck, trying not to nocite the small stream of blood oozing out from the pussy-couch, soaking our dear carpet.

INTERLUDE 1: DOLPHINS ON FIRE

FOR SOME TIME *we have to set the thorn bushes afire ourselves and shout the prophecies into the flames – poetic license– the basis of good neighborliness is not gossiping about the tenant above – not even in encomiums*

we wash beached dolphins – we rouge them and spritz some perfume on their skin – if the heart would have gills it wouldn't need to surface every time for air – always the same sight: something is pushing itself out our rib cage and there's very little time to measure some date rape drug for it

continents come and go on this planet – the burning choirboys always sing different songs and we've never seen the householder – now and then he flushes the toilet among the clouds – in the afternoon we smash the shower cubicles that we always made love in – the pieces are going to fit perfectly into the cracks where the render of the sky has fallen off

according to the news a thorn bush set itself aflame in the plaza and yelled obscenities at the tomfool shoppers before it collapsed into ashes – according to the news dolphins that doused themselves with oil and jumped out to land are suicide assassins and celebs – according to the news every out of tune piano is an assassin – a badly played Beethovencauses cancer in the brain –

according to the news the news is an assassin and the game who can see himself from a greater distance still played on a few square centimeters

burning buses rush on the roads with the ghosts of old prophets – they are always touring with their books written after their death – of course you'll need more to make a bestseller than dying in pain or produce the smell of roses on a bonfire – hear that? – the buriedpianos are still playing underground though their sheet music were thrown into the selective receiver and a fire prevention code was printed on them that shows how to by-pass hell in a few easy dance steps

"somehow people believe that after they die everything starts to work normally" the ghosts shake their heads "but that's not true you know – the chaos is even bigger after death – there's not even justice in the afterlife"

startling news – you can't get any better in the countryside – maybe one – that all the things that happened to you was just some kind of foreplay to reincarnate as a dead fish – maybe it isn't such a bad thing – to be a dead fish I mean – they do not complain though a lot of unfairness happens to them

we wash beached dolphins with gasoline – we rouge them and spritz some perfume on their skin then we wait maybe they are going to fuck or just do something interesting – the national geographic keeps the camera ready – a few ecofreaks are so excited that they drown themselves in the sea except the ones who complain about the water being to oily – it must have streamed down from above – what a son of a bitch householder lives overhead – at least he didn't ring the bell for the rent yet – so we smash the shower cubicles that we always made love in – the pieces are going to fit perfectly into the cracks...

of course you can't plan anything properly on this level – the pieces we made are too tiny

you can see what a little puzzle we made – if they would fit we could piece a window together at the sky – looking through it we could see the selective receiver where we can throw our hearts – then we could wallow overhead all day long – the shower foam of the clouds would settle in our pubic hairs

so here we are standing on the beach waiting for some kindof forecast – we set the oily dolphins alight and zoom into their gawping mouths trying to solve their mute words in the smell of burning meat – then someone gapes his mouth pointing at the horizon – a giant heart surfaces from the sea – it beats once – then sinks back into the depths

PORN-FUGITIVES

THE TEENAGED BOY sneaks into his room, and closes the door excitedly. From under his pillow he pulls out the porn magazine he found last week in the attic. To his surprise, when he opens it, only blank pages yawn back at him. And soon, he hear the sounds of moaning coming from under his bed. Looking down, he discovers the tiny pornstars – miniature, naked people are having sex on the floor everywhere, in all kind of poses. The boy panics. If his parents finds out this, he's fucked. So he gets a pickle jar, and tries to collect the small muscular men and silicone breasted women. He manages to capture a few, but the others are too fast: a couple in missionary pose runs away on four legs and four hands, just like a spider – they crawl up on the wall, and disappear in a crack.

It's all just a bad dream – decides the boy, and he goes to bed. In the morning, waking up, he finds a tiny woman kneeling on his forehead, smiling for an invisible camera, while a small dude stands before her and jerks his cum onto her face. The boy sweeps them off, and jumps out of the bed. He finds that the inseparable couple still in missionary pose spun a jelly-like web made of their juices – small flies squirm in them, the couple swoops down on a shiny sperm-string, and begin to eat the insects, the filmy wings crack between their perfect, white teeth. The boy looks away with disgust, his eyes stare a woman at his night-stand: she lays on the digital alarm clock, moaning, sliding a dildo between her legs. The boy steps closer, and a word, like a heavy stone, falls out of his mouth: "Mom?"

It's really her, but she's much younger. The boy grabs up the porn magazine, searching for a date. He just realizes, it's nearly twenty years old. And the woman just looks like his mother two decades ago. His stomach clutches. Picking up a hankie, he tries to cover the tiny naked body, but his mother crawls out, smiles and winks at him, and she slides the dildo in her ass.

"Now what?" sighs the boy, but he doesn't have any time to think it over, a voice from the kitchen calls: "Breakfast is ready!"

*

He sits at the table with a confused look. His mother stands beside the gas-cooker, wearing an apron, with a big button and a sign: Want service? Just push the button. If nothing happens, serve yourself.

"Good morning, hun!" smiles the woman above the boiling oil. "What's the matter? You look worn-out. Haven't you slept well?"

The boy simply can't face her. He mutters something, while gazing at the empty white porcelain plate in front of him. Soon, a table-fork enters his field of view, with a ten inch long fried black fly at it's end. It falls into his plate. Looking at it's legs, that stand up like antennas, the boy pushes away the food, saying:

"Can I eat it later? I'm not really hungry right now," he moans. His mother doesn't answer, she just stands there and frowns. When the boy runs out of the kitchen, back to his room, she yells: "What's wrong? Are you sick?"

"I'm fine!" answers the kid, trying not to vomit while watching his tiny mother on the night stand sucking the dildo that she just pulled out of her ass.

✳

The boy decides, that some way or other he gets rid of the small porn stars. He grabs a cellophane tape, an empty shoe box, then he fishes out a used hanky from under his bed, and puts it in the middle of the room as a bait. The tiny porn models crawl out from the cracks of the wall, from the corners, sniffing in the air. They gather around the hanky with a hungry look on their face, scratching down the old, dried sperm. They eat, and don't recognize, it's a trap. When all the little perfect bodied nude models are around the hanky, the boy drops the shoebox on them, capturing the little intruders.

"Gotcha!" he laughs. Lifting it up a bit and pushing his hand into the box, he grabs out a red haired girl. Putting some cellophane tape on her, he sticks her back to one of the blank pages of the magazine. Then he pulls out another model.

After a few minutes, the magazine is populated again. The kid looks away shamefacedly, seeing that in his hurry, he taped some of the models back to the page in a rather unfortunate way. The cellophane tape has covered some of their faces, these unlucky ones are drowning and squirming, then their bodies stiffen, as they die.

The only naked porn star left in the shoebox is his mother. The boy looks down at her and back to the magazine with tearful eyes.

"Why haven't you ever told me?" he asks, but the small woman doesn't pay any attention to him, she just moans as she tries to fist herself. Then the boy sighs, and closes the magazine. The models inside are whimpering, as he pushes it back to it's place – under his pillow. He'll throw it out, he decides, but first, he must take care of his mom. But what can he do with her? He can't just glue back her into the magazine. And he can't just let her free either, he would die in shame, if someone saw his mom like this. He could keep her – in an ant farm or a cage, but then he would have to face her mother's shame every day.

"Just get rid of her!" a voice tells in his head. So he picks her up, and walks out of the room.

"I'm sorry mother!" he whispers, holding her over the toilet. The lilliputian woman doesn't seem to understand what is happening to her, the waves of orgasm carry away her look, as a tiny vibrator's silent buzzing fills the bathroom. Then splash, she falls into the toilet. The vibrator discharges with micro-sparks. His little mother tries to crawl out from the porcelain-pit, but the boy pushes the flush lever, and the vortex spins and pulls her down.

CAYMAN–CRADLE

THE HUNTERS ARE dragging a behemoth dead crocodile into the village. The rope around the reptile creaks painfully. The heavy body of the animal scoops a trench in the mud. Bloody storm water swirls in it. Celebrating villagers greet the killers, throwing flower petals around them. The petals turn into butterflies and disappear in the sky.

It's been a long time since the villagers had seen a predator this big—the children keep touching its dark, scaly skin, gazing at its sharp teeth. The whole animal is about fifteen feet long; cruelty peels out of its dead, stiff eyes like dry rust.

Then something strange happens: the faint belly of the animal unexpectedly heaves and bloats. A hole appears in it. The bloody tip of a knife sticks out from the wound and begins to broaden the crack. The children hide behind their mothers' backs, and the dark hunters point their sharp lances towards the crocodile.

The Alligatorhunter crawls out from the reptile's body and stares at the natives with crazy, distant eyes. He shakes himself like a wet dog, and pieces of insides and drops of blood fly over. He raises his glittering knife and starts yelling—the exultant shout gives the tribe a jump—and in the distance, monkeys fall from the trees and leeches puke blood back into their victims.

"You fools!" The white hunter laughs. His face boils like the tainted river. "This beast is all mine! So you think you killed it? Oh, you're wrong! I crawled into the ugly animal three days ago, and since then, I've been constantly destroying it from the inside! What's more, I finally found its soul, and now it's all mine! Come on, take it from me! Take it, if you dare!"

The Alligatorhunter jumps to the ground. The villagers stare at him with frightened eyes. Even the most muscular hunters are afraid of this man, because they have heard so many rumors about him. It is said that the mosquito-disease lurks inside this white devil's veins. It is well known that some mosquitoes suck the dreams out from the skulls of people at night, puking back dark insect-thoughts instead. The natives have seen many people go crazy with this illness over the years. The afflicted would wake up in the morning, just like nothing had happened. Later, they would begin to buzz, simulating the sound of the mosquitoes, and in the end, the mad bastards would sharpen a lance and stab everyone in sight. This jungle has many nasty surprises: trees with piranha leaves, killer tendrils and predator orchids, which diffuse the smell of wet genitals to allure young lovers and gnaw off the flesh from their bones. And of course, there were the shape-shifter plants which can turn into attractive women and hunt men. There's a horrible report about a native man, who lived years with a shape-shifter woman without knowing what she was. You should have seen that female! She even birthed the poor guy's children. But everything ended when the mother began to slowly eat her babies. You see, when she was breastfeeding them, her nipples turned into sharp prickles which sent thorns into the children's palates. From outside, she looked like a normal mother feeding her infants, but in fact, she sucked the blood out of her kids, who became more and more sleepy.

So the green stomach of the jungle consumes the humans—mostly the white visitors—very fast. But the Alligatorhunter survived somehow over the years. He was an albino ghost, a bad spirit; a dead woman whispers in his head without intermission. It was his bride, who was eaten by a crocodile many years ago.

"Here you go, dogs!" The Alligatorhunter laughs, pointing at the carcass with his dirty finger. "You can have what it has left! Bzzz!"

Then he hops away and disappears behind the trees, squishing and killing tiny lizards with his heavy boots, sucking the colors out from the chameleons sitting on the branches. The animals became transparent and fell down to the ground.

The villagers spit towards the white man, and then they look at the crocodile. It's almost empty. It seems like the bastard has eaten all of its insides. The smell is unbearable. But of course, this made their job easier. The natives didn't wish to eat the animal. They wanted to offer up a sacrifice for the River God, and an eviscerated crocodile is just what they needed. So the villagers bring a crying Negro baby, holding it up high, while some women try to quiet down his screaming, whining mother.

The ritual is lead by a snake-masked man. To his command, the villagers lay the kicking baby into the disemboweled reptile. Then women arrive with needles made of bones and yarn made of hair, and they begin to stitch the giant wound shut.

Soon, the crocodile—with the living infant in its womb—is thrown into the river. The snake-masked wizard kneels in the slop, chanting, asking the River God to bless their hunts in the future. Hunters run in the forests, feeling the Braille of wounds—touching the bloody cracks of the animals and reading out words from them. Young children sit around them and listen to what the carcasses say. They always tell stories about the life of the animal or tales about the dangers in the forest, like the predator wind which chases the living beings through the jungle. It can tear down the flesh from their bones and blow away the small flame of the soul.

The powdered carbon of the night peels on to the world. The louver boards of nightmares spring open. The river finally spits out the long carried crocodile body onto the shore. A beautiful naked woman steps out from a bush, holding a sharp lance before her wild face, and she looks at the carcass. She hears stifled cries coming from the reptile. The woman discovers the stitches in the animal's belly, and she cuts the wound open with the weapon. Then, she picks up the baby and smiles. The child keeps kicking the night with his soft feet, crying as loudly as he can. The woman offers the little boy one of her round, black breasts. The baby begins to suck the fat nipple, which turns into a sharp prickle between his lips.

Far away, the Alligatorhunter sits on the shore on a throne made of reptile bones and skin. Sometimes he coughs up crocodile voodoo dolls and begins to poke them with a knife. The sounds of painful squirms fill the night. His long lost bride whispers in his head: "My dear husband! I walked so much in the other world that my legs have frayed. Now I'm crawling on my pelvis, which lessens and lessens, too. I've been dead for a long time; please leave the crocodiles in peace! I threw flower petals into their mouths. Sometimes, I turn into a tiny bird and peck out my own remains from their teeth. There's a door in every crocodile, my love, and if you open and look behind it, you will find the god of this river!"

The Alligatorhunter tries to understand her words, but he can't listen. The ugly buzzing of the mosquitoes echoes in his skull. He looks around him and sees fish skeletons stuck in the slop. They glow with green lights in the dark like fallen, poisoned stars.

THE OTHER HALF

THE MAGICIAN HAS a crush on his beautiful assistant, but so far, he doesn't ask her out on a date. Later, a great opportunity comes along, when the old "sawing a woman in half" trick goes somehow wrong, and he has to conciliate her. So he asks her out to dinner. The assistant says yes straight away, blushing. Now the only question is, which part of the woman the magician should take out tonight. He would seem too pushy if he chooses the lower half, so he eventually drives the upper half to a restaurant.

There's a strange, awkward mood around the table. Every bite of food the assistant swallows falls out from her bisected body. The magician tries to look away, kicking the undigested bits under the table, but soon, he can't bare it any longer and takes the woman home. There, the assistant winks and tells him he can take her lower part into the bedroom, if he wants to. She doesn't have to say it twice. After a wondrous night, the magician asks the upper part for another date.

But as the weeks go by, he begins to get more and more bored by the upper half. After a few more dinners, he gets fed up with the food stains on his shoe. At the same time, he and the lower part of the woman gets along better and better in bed. The man arranges secret meetings with the lower half, but the other half presses for dates, too. Time to time, he carries the upper half to the restaurant. He orders some food and a bottle of wine, and then he excuses himself to the restroom. He sneaks home to the lower part before the torso would start putting food in her mouth. After an occasion like this, when he's romping with the lower half in bed, someone knocks at his door.

He dresses and opens it. To his surprise, it is the upper half of the assistant—she's drunk, and the waiter carried her here. She clings on the man like a spider monkey.

"We're here for my pussy. I promised this guy he can have it." She burps and nods at the waiter.

"You can't do this! We…" The magician's look glances off the girl. "All right. She's… it's in the bedroom."

The excited waiter puts the woman's upper side into an armchair, and then he rushes into the bedroom. A key turns in the lock, and the magician begins to pace with a resigned visage. He sighs, and then he fixes a glass of wine for the upper half of the girl. She drinks it. Some of the fluid flows out from underneath her, onto the furniture.

"You have no heart," says the woman, rolling the glass between her fingers. The magician tries to lighten the mood with a joke.

"But I have. I keep it in one of my trick pockets." He slips his fingers under his shirt. To his surprise, he feels something soft and hairy between his skin and the cloth. He pulls out a drowned rabbit. He shakes the dead animal, and then he throws it into the corner of the room and fills a glass for himself.

THE WOMB-TAILOR

THAT DAY, THE tailor boy is called again to help with another birth. According to the elders, the evil horses from the sky were responsible for the black magic that impregnated every female in the village all at once on a mysterious night. And it only took two weeks for everyone to deliver the fruit of their wombs.

Normally, an old, blind lady helped out with the labors in the village, but after a flaming thorn bush jumped in her window and killed the old witch, the job was left to the tailor boy, who had some smattering of childbirths. But what surprises awaited this young man! A celestial curse-pregnancy is never like a usual: the girls began to give birth to the strangest things possible. One woman delivered a sewing machine to the world that stitched the feathers to the birds, the birds to the sky, and finally the sky to the souls of lovers. Another girl wasn't this lucky, a giant kitchen knife was growing inside her womb, and when the time came, it sliced her birth canal in two. Fortunately, the tailor boy always had some needle and yarn in his pocket, but after some time he decided it will be much easier for everyone if he starts with a caesarean section. So he began slicing up the girls. Once, balloons filled with helium flew out from an open wound, another time, he found a large gaping catfish in the uterus. It was a nasty job picking it out, the skin was so sloppy that the fish slipped through the boy's fingers, splashing back into the bloody hole over and over again. He had to knot a hook onto a string, and fish out the animal, while the mother was shouting in his ears,"Look at the little bastard, ouch, he has a moustache just like his father's, I tell ya', ouch! But how could it be his? I open my legs for him only twice a year, just when he's dancing on the ceiling with the pain of blue balls! Ouch! But first, I order him to bring mirrors! Lots of lots of mirrors! So he can admire my body from every angle! And after he praises every inch of me, I order him to count all of my hairs. So the whole procedure takes about four days! Ouch! Oh no, no, I haven't opened my thighs for him this year, it can't be his brat, I assure ya!"

"Stop squirming so much, or I'll accidently leave this hook in you, it will be a fine job pissing it out!" growls the tailor boy, then he looks aside and his eyes make a teacup explode.

That night, they cook the fish for supper, and the villagers put their heads together over the soup to discuss this whole birth situation.

"The Celestial Stable!" whispers an old woman. "From where the evil spirits come! At first glimpse, they are just like any other horse you ever saw. But if you give them a second look and stare in to their eyes... you'll see the melting faces of people, who's souls they've stolen. If you'd cut their skin with a knife, screams would ooze out from those wounds... Beware the horses from the sky!"

The saw-teeth of goosebumps. You could cut out a tree with the children. The villagers stave off every horse from the neighborhood, letting them out from the stables, not even looking into their eyes anymore, they beat them with sticks, watching them disappearin the line of the horizon. The village border now is full of sauntering stallions rooting around in the snow with their snorting noses, eating the pages of thrown out books, and sad ghosts chase each other in the clouds of their breath.

The next day, the tailor boy is called again, to help with another birth. They lead the boy into a room, where a fifteen years old girl is bathing in her own sweat. Her parents are standing next to her bed, crunching their skinny hands, broken butterfly wings fall out from under their nails.

"Don't worry! The procedure is easy, like making wine from shirt-sleeves." Says the tailor boy, and with his self-confidence, he has already won the heart of the parents. The mother boils some water, the father takes out a bottle of palinka.

The tailor boy looks at the girl's giant belly, saying, "Place your bets, folks, I say it will be a bucket full of stones! Or a cage, with a mad rooster in it!"

But no more jokes, the boy starts to work. his scissors fly out of his haversack, they grow and grow, and when the instrument is

91

large enough, the tailor sits on it, riding it like a horse, yelling, "Giddy up, free that child!"

He flies up and down in the room while the mother claps a jolly folk rhythm. The father pours some flaming alcohol into his daughter's mouth, who begins to yell, "Countess, oh my dear countess, you left your beautiful hair in the cabinet last summer! I preserved it for you, blowing my nose into it only once or twice! Oh, the frame of mind is more than good, the bathtub is full of prayer books, can't wait to go and wash my sins down!"

"No time for illusions, let's do it quick!" the boy encourages the young mother, cutting her open. The blood sprays biblical scenes onto the wall.

"Oh, but it's empty!" yells the tailor angrily, his hand moving around in the hole. "There's just thin air in it. What a scam!"

The father slaps his knees, saying, "Maybe the baby's invisible! Don't forget, we're dealingwith black magic!"

"Maybe, maybe." murmurs the tailor, but he doesn't really believe in it. "Well, you shouldn't take the risk! You should raise the child, or just pretend that you are raising something. Rather raise the nothing, than leave something unseen unraised."

Cotton balls gather in swarms, like flies, they buzz, drinking up all the blood in the room they can find. The family promises a meal for the tailor boy, and while the food boils, they sit him down on to an old armchair. As soon as he puts down his butt, the furniture begins to cry. Jumping up, the tailor finds a large bulge under him, so he takes out his scissors, and cuts up the textile. Inside he discovers a crying pink baby.

"Ah, here's that prodigal son!" he cheers, fishing out the child. He brings him to the young mother. "Neither a bucket of stones nor a cage with a rooster, it's a real boy, I tell ya!'

He hands him over, the tears of the girl washes the baby. The newborn keeps reaching his fingers, he hooks his eyes into her mother's gaze. It must be her imagination, but the girl catches a glimpse of her own melting, screaming face in the baby's pupil.

After eating, the tailor boy sits on his giant scissors. He lifts and flies away over the snowy roofs, yelling, "Behold, here comes the womb tailor! I'll nose out every fetus, and throw them into the deep water of the world!"

A red swarm of used cotton balls follow him.

In the village border, loud neighs scare away the crows that leave their thin legs standing in the snow. A brown horse arrives, snorting angrily. It ascends, and disappearsamong the grey winter clouds.

That night, giant sperm cells rain from the sky. Like long white worms, they squirm on the roofs, then crawl inside the houses to impregnate the sleeping girls.

February. February. All stillness is temporary.

SLAVES IN A CLOSET

THE GIRL DISCOVERS that the boy she moved in with is secretly a slaveholder. While hovering, she finds a coffee plantation under the bed. And when she wants to iron the sheets, she discovers thin, beaten Negros in the closet. She realizes this is something she must discuss with her boyfriend.

Soon, her lover arrives home – riding a muscular thoroughbred, a whip sways back and forth on his side.

They sit at the kitchen table to drink their coffee, and the girl tells her boyfriend about her discovery. She also says, that she can't commit her heart to a slaveholder; her parents raised her as a liberal. The boy listens for a while, then he asks: "But the coffee's good, isn't it?"

The girl wants to say something, but she can't deny that.

"Maybe they would do the cleaning and the washing too, if I would teach them." adds the boy. The girl doesn't say a word. She just drinks her coffee. She stays mute for the next couple of days. She shuts her ears at nights, when her boyfriend crawls out from the bed, and disappears in the closet. But still, she can hear the crying, and the cracking sound of the whip.

In the morning, she pours fresh beans into the coffee-grinder. It must be her imagination, but she sees the coffee beans as tiny crying Negro babies. Her eyes glimmer with tears, when she turns the machine on. Then she begins to cry, as the sound of bone cracking fills the room.

INTERLUDE 2: GLOOMY SUNDAY

NO ONE THOUGHT the celebrity chef of the weekend cookery program was really the leader of a suicide cult. Just after finishing a sauce she showed the housewives how to stick their heads into a gas oven, to get relief from everyday pain, and thousands of husbands found their wives dead in the kitchen. Everyone started to suspect.

But of course even suicide cults aren't what they used to be. You join one, waiting for them to carry you into a field where a big bald man walks around with a six-shooter between his praying hands, kissing cyanide capsules into your mouth. Instead, they all just sit in armchairs, eating fast food, not doing any exercise, saying that the most efficient way to kill yourself is eating microwave popcorn. Even a shot to the head isn't always effective. Sometimes the bullet doesn't go through the bone; it just runs around inside the skull and flies out the other side. That's why better schools teach children that they should look around carefully before blowing their brains out.

"I've seen many people who weren't brave enough to pull the trigger, but have never seen anyone eat popcorn with a shaking hand." A fat cult follower burps, proudly showing his terrible cholesterol results. The company cancels the cooking program, desperate housewives exchange old recipes on the black market, while a twelve year old girl is interviewed on a new talk show. She was raped by her father and the blood on her blanket formed the face of Christ. The dad hugs his little girl, an APPLAUSE sign lights up, but the viewers switch to another channel and the ratings drop. The talk show host opens a tiny door in his microphone and fishes out a cyanide capsule. The channel gave it to him; it's all in the contract, you see.

After a week, they start a reality show starring the suicide cult members, so we can watch how they poison themselves day after day. Our new, lazy spiritual leaders burp up new slogans, for instance "Life is the new suicide." Well, Sunday's programs always sucked, so no one stays at home. A small crowd gathers around McDonald's to watch the young girl marry her father. They pass around French fries and cola, saying it's the body and the blood of The Savior (and yes, it's sugar free). They remember Christ, who was strong enough not to swallow the cyanide capsule hidden in his crucifix. The moment we've all been awaiting finally arrives. The voice of a bored worker comes from

Ronald McDonald's plastic statue: "Do you take this man to be your husband?" The girl with the bloody blanket on her head

looks at her father, and when she says no, the crowd is outraged,
picking up pavers from the parking lot. The good old stoning
lures some hungry cameras.

Stones fly like the bullets God once shot into his head, but
didn't kill him—they just ran around inside his skull and flew out
the other side. They're floating now in space—we've
overpopulated one of them, and now we're searching for a new
one. Our little robots carry HD cameras on them as we switch and
switch between planets. Then we switch to another channel,
where an infomercial pitchman tries to sell us a new detergent.
To demonstrate its effectiveness, he washes out the blood-Christ
from the little girl's white blanket. Then he advises us that we
should also try drinking it, to get relief from everyday pain. Who
would have ever suspected this nice infomercial pitchman?

WET DREAMS

THE GIRL IS watching her sleeping boyfriend at night. Suddenly
she discovers a small door on the boy's forehead. When she opens
it, and peeps inside, she notices laughing girls, running on a
beach totally nude. She becomes jealous, and starts to shake her
partner. As she jolts the sleeping boy, the little nude girls fall out
from the boy's forehead, on to the bed, and then onto the floor.
The girl treads them with anger.

Eventually, the boy and the girl reconcile, and they make love, while little red puddles are drying on the carpet.

HORSES FROM THE SKY ATE HER SUGAR LUMP EYES

THE GIRL STANDS at the window with a slingshot in her hand. She scratches out her eyeballs and shoots them into the clouds, yelling, "Go! Go and see the world!"

Her eyes fly over the snowy roofs of the village, where birds stand aside to give them way. Finally, the eyeballs slam into the side of a sauntering cow in the village border. They sink deep under its skin, into its flesh, and a painful moo tears up the grey clouds on the sky.

"What a prisoner I am in this ugly house!" sighs the blind girl, cowering to the ground, hitting the old boards of the wooden floor with her weak little fists, trying to cry without eyes. "This whole village is just a cage. The world just grows and grows outside, while I'm shrinking here."

Hearing the noise, her stooped, old mother steps into the room. When she glimpses the deep, red pits where her daughters deep blue eyes use to glint, she screams: "Oh, you fool! Your beautiful eyepearls! Come on, stand up, you'll catch pneumonia down there! Lizards will build a nest into your throat, I tell you!"

"Enough, mother! Stop telling me what to do!" mutters the girl, but she's too weak to resist. Soon, her father arrives too and puts her in the bed, blanketing her.

"Stay there, young lady!" groans her dad. "You know you are such a weak little child, if you would go to the kitchen, the spoons would crawl under your skin! If you would step on to the doorsill, maggots would bite into your toenails! Ugly germs lurk in this world, and even dewy air can destroy your beautiful paper-skin!"

"My weakness exists only in your head!" answers the girl, but they cook a soup from the potty, and the hot liquid seals her mouth.

It's afternoon. The family is pouring coffee, boiled from black flies, into small cups. When they throw the sugar cubes into the streaming drink, the father recognizes his daughter's sweet look in one of the lumps. It gives him an idea. He steps to his daughter's bed, and drops sugar cubes into the girl's empty red eye sockets one into each.

"Now look at that! My daughter is so beauteous!" He cheers, pointing at the girl's new sugar-eyes. She just blinks and blinks, but still, she can only see the moving insides of a cow.

"By choice, I would put her into a show-case, and just gaze her from dawn to fall. Of course, now and then, I would wipe the spider webs off of her, but that's all – the prettiest birds need to be secured in a cage!"

Night falls. Bad luck oozes out from the horseshoes. The father lies in his bed, his long beard floats around his face as he snores. In his forehead, like a tiny ballerina, spins his shrunken, two inch long daughter. Her toes nearly touch the wrinkled, old skin, it's like she's floating between her fathers closed eyes. The sugar cubes are shining in her eyesockets.

"Oh, father, dear father!" moans the girl. "I have begged and begged for that ugly cow to give me back my eyes, or just puke them out and kick them far away, but it's such an evil and witless animal! At daylight, I almost accept my cage, but at night time, father, I would bite your throats, and bath in your blood! Doesn't every animal feel the same about their keepers? All birds hate fowlers."

Her sugar eyes cry sweet honey on to her father's mouth. She just cries and cries, until the man can't swallow any more and he begins to choke from the golden liquid.

"Father... Oh, father..." cries the girl. The old man squirms in his bed, rumpling the sheets with his kicking legs. Then he dies. A wind arrives, picking up the girl. It carries and puts her down onto her mother's forehead, and soon the honey fills her mouth too.

Door handles made of dead bees – rotting feathers in the pillow, somewhere in the night a long sausage, like a deadly snake, coils around a steak hammer. The blind girl keeps prodding the walls, and soon, she finds the door – crawling outside into the freezing night, she leaves her footsteps in the snow.

"How sweet is the air, how big is the world!" she yells. Her long, blonde hair reaches up and tickles the clouds' bellies. The sky laughs up two flying horses, which begin to chase the girl from above.

"Look, what an ugly pale mole crawled out from her hole!" neighs one of them.

"Don't be so rude, Freckles, look, she brought us presents!" They slope downward, and kick the blind girl with their hooves, who falls on to her back.

"Bon à petite!" whinnies Freckles, biting out one of the sugar cubes from the screaming girl's face.

"The lord's supper can't be better!" says the other, the sugar crackles between its teeth.

"Such a sweet girl, I hope she doesn't catch a cold!" laughs Freckles, coughing dark worms into her face.

"A little chill not ever killed someone!" tells the other. Then they spring to the air, and disappear in the sky.

"Oh, father. Oh, mother." stutters the girl, watching the insides of the sleeping cow, trying to read out her fortune. "The ugly germs found me, like you always said they would. My throat… It hurts. And fever set my thoughts on fire. I wish I had just stayed in my room, I wish you were here to take care of me…"

The girl doesn't stand up, she just lies there, as if she were in her comfy little bed. The snow begins to fall. Soon, a cold blanket grows around her body.

When morning arrives, she's just a bulge, a puckering on the white canvas. Her eyes inside of the cow are not glinting anymore, they are motionless marbles. The cowbell rings sadly on the animal's neck, like it wants to call the villagers together for a funeral. But no one comes; everyone stays inside their warm, comfy homes. In the sky, the old boards of Heaven's wooden floor crack, as a ghost keeps knocking on it with its weak little fists from beneath.

OLD TRICKS

IN THE MORNING, a salesman greets me at the door. He's not willing to leave until I watch what his vacuum cleaner is capable of. Eventually, I let him in to do his work. He carries a giant suitcase; I assume the machine is inside. But when he opens the case, a wounded woman crawls out from it. Her head is bleeding; the left arm hangs motionless beside her injured body. She looks like someone who got hit by a car.

"Please, call an ambulance!" the woman whimpers, but the salesman kicks her in the ankle.

"It's the newest model, you'll see what it's capable of, watch! Come on, clean!" What could the woman do? She begins to crawl on the floor, moaning painfully as the broken bones crack inside her body, and puts every shag pile she finds into her mouth. She chokes and coughs, while trying to swallow them. Blood is dripping onto my carpet.

"That's enough, I'm calling the police!" I say.

"There's no need for it, if you don't like the product, then I'll just leave!" he stutters, grabbing the woman by her legs, dragging her out from the house. Outside stands his car its front is damaged. I know there's only one way now to save the woman.

"Wait, I'll buy!" I yell, and the salesman begins to smile. As I give him the money, I curse myself for falling for the good old "hit a woman, and sell her as a vacuum cleaner" trick. The car drives away, and I call the ambulance. As they put the injured woman on a stretcher, the ambulance man asks if I got a warranty card. When I say no, they shake their heads and leave.

Returning to my house, I watch the blood stains on the carpet. How will I clean all this mess up? Soon, someone rings my door. It's the salesman again, this time offering a stain-remover. As I give him the money, I curse myself for falling for the good old "hit a woman, sell her as vacuum cleaner, who will mess up the carpet, so we can sell our stain-remover" trick.

PLASTICAT SURGERY

SOMETIMES, AS A favor, I perform cosmetic surgery on my friends' animals. Well, I don't have a license, or proper tools for this, and not even a clean operating room, of course, but I have many, many clients. Most of them want their pets to look younger, or want them to have longer tongues, maybe less protruding ears, perhaps prettier tails.

But today, the old neighbor lady rang my bell with a fat cat and an old photo in her hands. She wanted her pet to be more look like his dead husband. I gazed at the vintage black and white snapshot, measuring the face of a young soldier, his perky mustache, then I looked at the dull cat, and I nodded. It was a huge mistake. The surgery was a harder task than I imagined. I was carving the face of the cat for hours and hours, but no matter how hard I tried, it wasn't anything like the soldier in the end. Its head was a messy, red mass. In my final despair, I picked up some yarn and a needle, and sewed the photo to the animal's head. I also tied a toy gun to its back. The lady picked up her pet with a grim look on her face.

"It doesn't look like him at all." she said, and rushed out.

On the next day, I tried to placate her with a box of chocolates. I rang her bell. I heard some kind of army music coming from the house. Wild trumpets. The cat opened the door. It said: "My wife's not home."

But it took the chocolates, and slammed the door in my face.

FUEL

I NOTICE A strange symptom, so I decide to consult my doctor. My urine smells like gasoline. The doc doesn't believe me, so I have to produce a sample in his office. Puckering his brows he tells me: "Well, I admit. This really smells like fuel. But I'm gonna send this sample to the lab, we should wait for the results to come back."

A few days pass, and I'm still waiting. Then the doc calls, and tells me that the sample was lost, and I should bring another one to his office. More this time. Then this happens again. And again.

Later, the doc takes off for a few days, and I start to suspect that all the piss I gave him landed not in the lab, but in his car's fuel tank. I call his cell phone. He denies it, of course.

My friends are beginning to act weird too. There's not a day, when one of them doesn't ask me to come over for a drink. And when I ask them about the bathroom after a few beers, the answer is always the same: "Sorry, bro, broken pipe, use this can instead."

I stop visiting them, but I also can't go home anymore. Someone broke into my apartment last night, and packed my fridge full of drinks. I'm sauntering in the streets. Not drinking a single gulp. But strangers come to me, asking if they can buy me a drink. I must escape from the city. Faceless people follow me all day, catheter tubes quiver between their fingers. I woke up drunk. Someone must have poured beer down my throat, while I was sleeping in the alley.

I totter to my doc's house, spitting profanities and I piss down the corner of his house. A few drops land on my trousers too. Then I light a cigarette.

CONFETTI TEARS

THE BOY DISCOVERS a book deep in the closet. The Magical World of Origami – the title says. He opens it. The first page shows how to fold a lifelike pigeon. He grabs a piece of paper, and follows the instructions. When he's done, to his surprise, the bird flies out from his hands and out in the open window.

He gets excited, and turns to another page. This time, he folds a deer. When he finishes, the animal stretches it's long, thin legs, and begins to scud up and down the room. The boy then creates a hunter – a crabby looking paper guy, who immediately points his gun at the origami deer, and shoots it. A loud bang echoes through the room, and the animal falls to the ground. Real blood oozes out from the tiny torn paper hole.

The door opens and the boy's girlfriend enters the room. She screams and tries to take the book from the boy's hand with a worried look on her face, like if it was something the boy shouldn't see. He jumps back, and turns to the other page. It shows, how to fold a lifelike boyfriend. The paperboy on the picture looks just like him.

There's a lot of silence that afternoon. At night, the girl hugs the boy from behind, and whispers in his ear: "What if I folded you from paper? I still love you!"

The boy sighs. They make love – the boy's paper penis soaks, as he enters her girlfriend. It dries by morning. He wakes up all crumpled. The little hunter still runs up and down in the house, shooting tiny paper bullets into the corners. The boy is now standing in front of the mirror, examining himself. He begins to unfold his arm, and discovers word written on the paper. Bread. Cheese. Sausage. He can't believe his love folded him from glued shopping lists and bills. What a shame.

He steps to the open window and jumps out. But instead of hitting the ground, a fresh wind picks up his light body, and carries him over the city. His blue confetti-tears keep streaming from his eyes, and they fall down onto the passerby's' heads.

They brush the confetti out of their hairs, muttering: "Looks like someone's having a very good time."

THE WORKING OF WALLS

THIS IS HOW walls work:

Some guys play the nastiest game ever possible. When you walk on the street, they stand tightly to each other, blocking your way, telling you (look, even their mouths move together) that they are the wall, and you must break through if you want to continue your journey.

Of course, you try to by-pass them, but it's simply impossible, because they move so skilfully aligned together. You just stand there all helpless before them, when an idea hits you in the head. You quicklystep aside, next to the winger, pushing your shoulder to his, joining the line, saying, "We are the wall then."

The guys look confused. Then they nod, and repeat the sentence.

So you stand all in unison. Waiting for someone to arrive.

And this is how I work the walls:

There's a wide wall in front of me with a cavity in it. I'm deepening this little pit for quite a time now, hitting my head to the concrete again and again with the monotony of a metronome.

Yesterday I stopped, to size up the crater I have made.

I see someone's bleeding forehead in frontof me. Maybe it belongs to God.

AFTERWORD: THE DEATH OF ART

BLANK PAGES PLAYING tag in an empty alley – behind a dustbin the homeless watches this strange waltz – long forgotten writings, the ghosts of unfinished stories they are dead all right – a writer with his pen draws a straight line to his wrist – red ink spouts out from his hand – while the movie director hangs himself with a roll of film – small images stretch on his neck – they show the evolution of a smile which belongs to a half-hearted actress – she's at home now sitting in her bathtub still feeling the projector's heat on her face – swallowing the letters of a script with expensive wine – r, a, s, f, j, c – the hooked letters need at least two drams but when they go down the poison slowly begin to take effect – a scriptwiter's bitterness is deadly

a lifeline torn down from the palm – steady little string there where people who hanged themselves with it – in a studio the soul's untarnishable firework still sparks on the wet canvas

the painter works on his self-portrait after it's done he throws it on the fire and he himself turns into ashes with the picture – somewhere a ceramist forms and bakes his own heart then dashes the whole thing in to pieces while the graphic artist is drawing another nude – his pencil tears off the model's clothes – after that the skin and the flesh

black insects marching down from the score and devours the musician – his last scream is one enormous musical note – vehement connoisseurs try to chase it down – their long toad tongues dangling from their mouths and yes, there were people who hanged themselves with these – an architect destroys the city with a single upstroke – the writer just realizes that only with hooked letters can he catch a muse – …r, a, s, f, j, c… – the caught muses are squirming in the corner – silver scales keep dropping from their bodies – this is the only payment poets will ever get

"the happiness of every artist fits into my palm" says the homeless with no arms "when i had my hands i wrote beautiful pieces of poetry the poems were nesting under my nails i just had to snap with my fingers and rhymes were born"

there is a small drop of ink in the corner – it must escaped from the wound of a poet – a poem forms from it and begins its search to find the death of art – God knows why

INFO & ABOUT THE AUTHOR

ZOLTⓃN KOMOR WAS born in June 14, 1986. He lives in Nyⓘregyhⓘza, Hungary. He writes surreal short stories and published in several literary magazines (Caliban Online, Drabblecast, The Phantom Drift, Gone Lawn, etc.). His first English book, titled Flamingos in the Ashtray: 25 Bizarro Short Stories, was released by Burning Bulb Publishing in 2014.

Contact: **komorzoltan@gmail.com**

"Cayman-cradle" and "The Other Half" originally appeared in StrangeHouse Books' "Strange Story Saturdays", "Slaves in a Closet", and "Old Tricks" originally appeared in Bizarro Central's "Flash Fiction Friday", "Crotch-couch" and "Secret Skull House" originally appeared in "The Strange Edge Magazine", "The Violin-fishers", "The Wild Bull", "Gloomy Sunday" and „The Working of Walls" originally appeared in "Caliban Online, "Horses from the Sky Ate Her Sugar Lump Eyes" originally appeared in "TheNewerYork, "Fuel" originally appeared in "Chrome Baby, "Mall-head" and "Nipples of a Soda Automat" originally appeared in "The Breakroom Stories" online journal of audio fiction.

MorbidbookS is a grotesque Bizarro ballet where the most profane things occur. An impious and perverse dwelling of dark revulsion. A cozy cottage where torture porn and brutal bible tales are devised. A quiet place to relax and spin tales of depravity and wickedness. A halfway house for the disturbed where rules no longer apply. A safe haven for deviant serial killers to hatch their wretched schemes.

Bring your pets.

The tasty ones are always welcome.

WWW.MORBIDBOOKS.WORDPRESS.COM

Also available from ~MorbidbookS~

In Print & Kindle Editions:

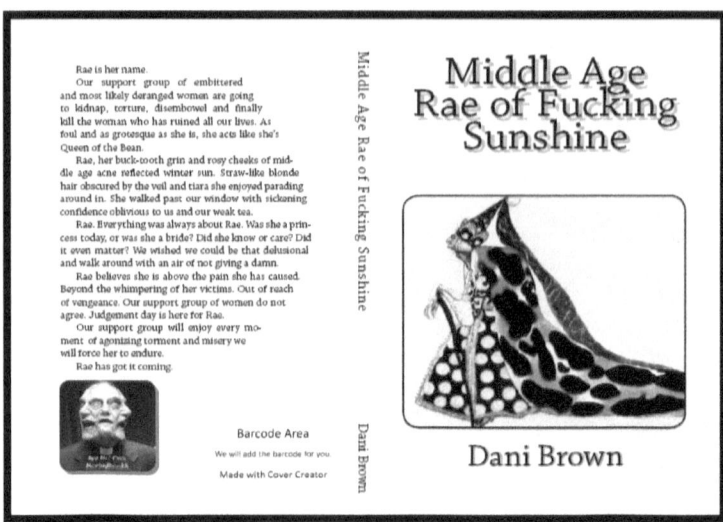

Rae is her name.

Our support group of embittered and most likely deranged women are going to kidnap, torture, disembowel and finally kill the woman who has ruined all our lives. As foul and as grotesque as she is, she acts like she's Queen of the Bean.

Rae, her buck-tooth grin and rosy cheeks of middle age acne reflected winter sun. Straw-like blonde hair obscured by the veil and tiara she enjoyed parading around in. She walked past our window with sickening confidence oblivious to us and our weak tea.

Rae believes she is above the pain she has caused. Beyond the whimpering of her victims. Out of reach of vengeance. Our support group of women do not agree. Judgement day is here for Rae.

Rae has got it coming.

"No! You will not move. You say I am a fucking clown, and so I will be. And I will fuck you until I can fuck you no more. And when I am done, perhaps I will take you down to the cattle car and watch while the other clowns fuck you one by one until you are so full that their juices run down your thighs. You will learn to show respect for me. For my art and my craft."

Pinning her hands to the bed, he entered her quickly and roughly. She screamed and spit in his face. He slapped her again and left her ear ringing as he wiped the spittle from her face and continued to pound her hard and fast.

"You hate clowns? Well you have a clown inside of you right now. How does that feel? A fucking clown is raping you and he'll continue to do it until it pleases him to stop."

115

~The hands of the girls were inside of each-others zip front grey boiler suits and they sat in the blood from where Sonny's face collided with the surface. The brunette had a finger smear of it next to her mouth.

"You two sluts put each other down and go tell Moira that Sonny's done. I'm coming in, just got a little business to attend to first."

As the two started to leave the big blond grabbed the shoulder of the red head and pulled her back.

"Not you Fire-Crotch, all this fucking blood has got me going."

She started to unbuckle the belt on her camouflage hot pants.

"Down you go, bitch!"

116

~Short stories from the Most Depraved Writer in Print. Dark and twisted tales of exquisite violence, rough tricks, narcotics consumption, evil ghosts and drug-snuffling demons. Evil grandfathers and animal-human hybrid clones. Morbid serial killer stalking night darkened hallways of an unsuspecting hospital. Life underground following the frozen apocalypse. Tales of ancient blood-thirsty vampires and Roman decadence. Enjoy all of the hardcore, dystopic, viscerally violent stories. Not for easily offended mamby-pambies. Dark fiction at its finest.

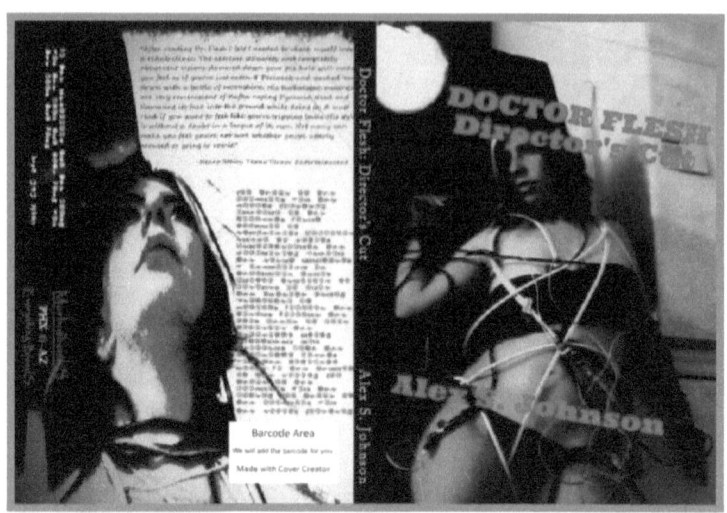

~From Alex S. Johnson, the author of Bad Sunset, Wicked Candy and The Death Jazz, comes a new vision in Bizarro horror. Imagine a TROMA film on meth and acid, one part cyberpunk, one part Franz Kafka, and three parts frankly unsuitable for a sane audience. "Will make you feel as if you've just eaten 8 Percocets and washed 'em down with a bottle of moonshine," says Necro Stein of Texas Terror Entertainment.

~**When the winds blew i felt them blowing through me,** when the land shook, it was my corpus that trembled. When the tides ebbed and flowed I became more shore and more sea. I was day and night as the sun and moon described the steps of their dancing within me. Just as I could see all the world at once, I was all of these things at once, and the motion of an entire world formed the foundation of my stillness.

I'd travelled through the Sphere of Glammeth, descended through the Guardian, and then through the Grey-Man, fallen through a hole that pierced all the worlds.

~**He had to have her the moment he saw her trachea ring.** Six months later she was his lovely wife. He performed his duties as a husband and she as a wife. He tolerated a house filled with references to her late first husband and the children they had together. He put up with her prudish ways. He waited. He was patient. He planned. He was adaptable. He was rewarded over the course of a week in her basement. He turned his perverse sexual fantasies of worms and maggots and her lovely crusty trachea ring into a gruesome reality.

~A dirty shameful devil of a secret...

Something that two men share. A legacy that will shock you to your very core. One that is created not out of madness, but of the purest desire. Take a vivid journey into the mind of the killer and his biggest fan. Do you believe in evil? See the knife plunge. Lap at the wounds. Do you still? There is no rational meaning or pretty words that will hide away the darkness that the words of this found journal creates. Inside is the real truth. And it can set you free. Watch all you want. Taste what you dare not have.

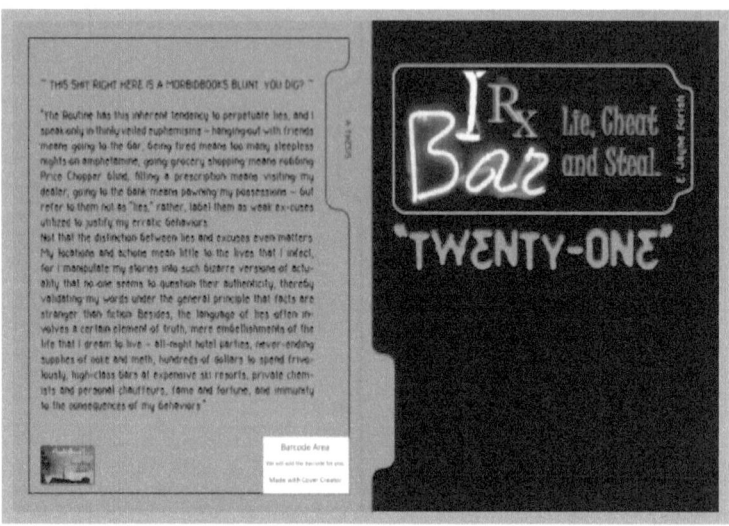

~"**The routine has this inherent tendency to perpetuate lies,** and I speak only in thinly veiled euphemisms — hanging out with friends means going to the bar; being tired means too many sleepless nights on amphetamine; going grocery shopping means robbing Price Chopper blind; filling a prescription means visiting my dealer; going to the bank means pawning my possessions — but refer to them not as "lies;" rather, label them as weak excuses utilized to justify my erratic behaviours.

~**I'm feeling down and dirty, feeling kind of mean,** so I give those fans my middle finger. Those poor bastards go nuts. My team looks at me in awe. My coach frowns and the opposing one begins to furiously scratch out new plays. I see our opponents and I almost feel sorry for the poor bastards. Their fans can't help them. Their coach can't help them. I'm going to run them off their own track in front of their own fans and there is not one thing they can do about it.

~**Humanity is the devil is a deconstructed nightmare mixing David Lynch and snuff movies.** The plot revolves around a central character, Seth, who is set about a crusade against humanity which, for him, represents pure evil. Through random killings he and his cronies try to accelerate the end of the world, in order to provoke and defeat the Demiurge, the false God that is ruling the earth. As in Burroughs, logical language is replaced here with cut–scenes – sometimes to be taken literally – that plunge the reader into an extreme experience.

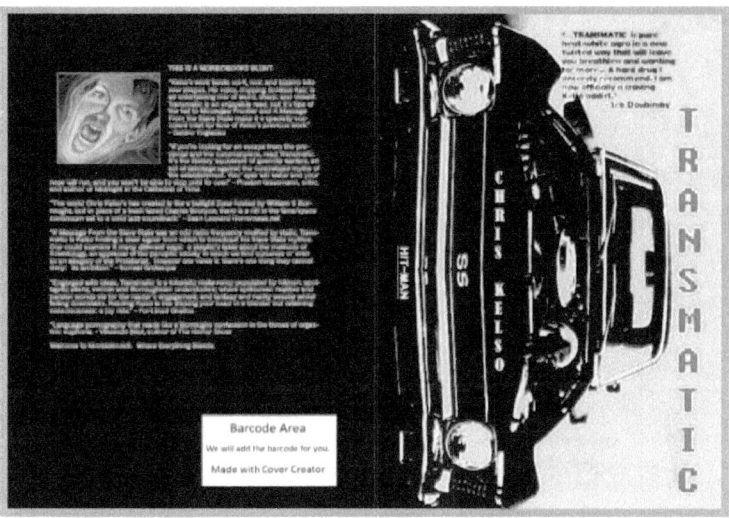

~"As a part-time hitman/ exterminator, Ignius Ellis's dream is to buy a candy-apple red Nova Supreme. In the process of trying to earn enough cash to make his dream come true he gets sucked into the rough world of Visitacion Valley, SF. When the tenants in his apartment complex reveal their various extracurricular activities this take an even more bizarre twist and Ellis soon becomes acquainted with the nightmarish Slave State dimension..."

~That's the last time she gets the bigger worm...

Once their flesh flakes away the angels collapse into puddles of hissing goop and withered petals blow into them hurried along by unseen winds. My spit looses its sweet taste to the black flavor of ash. The glowing birds in the bright orange sky burst into small sparkly novas. The sky itself weeps and tears, streaking down like a ruined painting as the dismal grey of life wheezes back before my eyes. I don't blink; praying silently for one last desperate sensation of the high. Lila feels it too. She writhes on the mattress next to me...

~Scary as ever.

He looked at her and grinned wickedly, the overcasting shadows of the outer corner of the stone wall, combined with the flickering light above them, created a deadly feature across the side of his face. He sees her lying helpless. He chuckled eerily, and instantly raised his hand. Her eyes widened to the sight of the gleaming sharp knife in his grasp. He even held it up for her to see it better. She stared up at him and then to the knife, panting in fear. Her heart pounded throughout her body as he chuckled once more saying deeply,

"Oh excellent. I've found you . . ."

~**Within these twisted and perverted pages**, Johnson manages to demolish clichés with a jaded finesse that I've personally never encountered in written form. Another apparent talent is his effortless deconstruction of pop-culture allegories and references as found in his story "Vampussy." No one is safe or spared from his dagger sharp sarcasm and wit.

While not without its flaws, my appreciation for this kind of talent and voice is what made his writing so fun to read, even if he might possibly be out of his ever-loving mind.

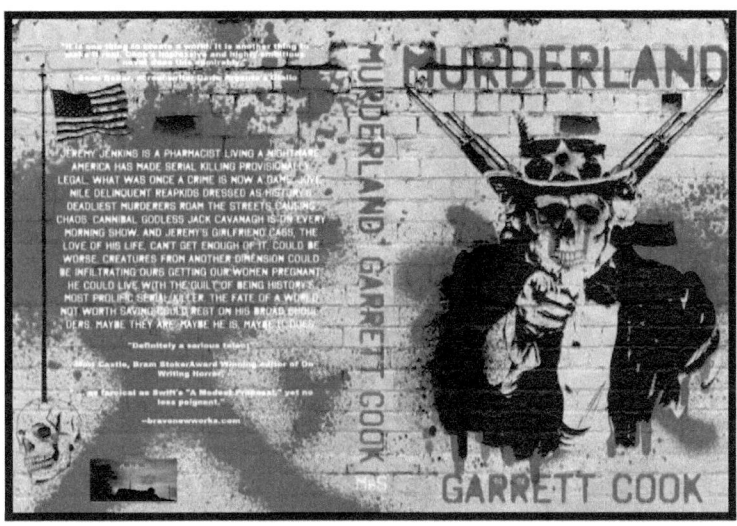

~In Garrett Cook's Murderland serial killers are idolized by society. Their deeds are followed obsessively by television pundits and the adoring public. A subculture has grown up around this phenomena, called "Reap." Laws are created to allow this activity to flourish, including designated "safe zones' where killers can practice their trade without fear of persecution. Fans of the top rated serial killers celebrate each new kill on social media and television. Programs glorify their deeds.

The culture of Murderland is violent and mirrors our own violent society and its decadent obsessions.

~**Born whole from the rectum of a dying patient, Morbid silently stalks the hospital's hallways,** heinously dispatching the most helpless of patients and in the most painfully repulsive of manners. In the meantime, in order to pay for his family and home that includes his ghost step-father Sammy and his pet aborted fetus Chip, Westphal has to ingest mounds of dangerous narcotics to get through his night shifts. Barely hanging on to his Care Tech gig by his fingernails, the last thing Westphal needs is to be accused of Morbid's evil deeds. You, on the other hand, simply seek some solace from all Your diseases.

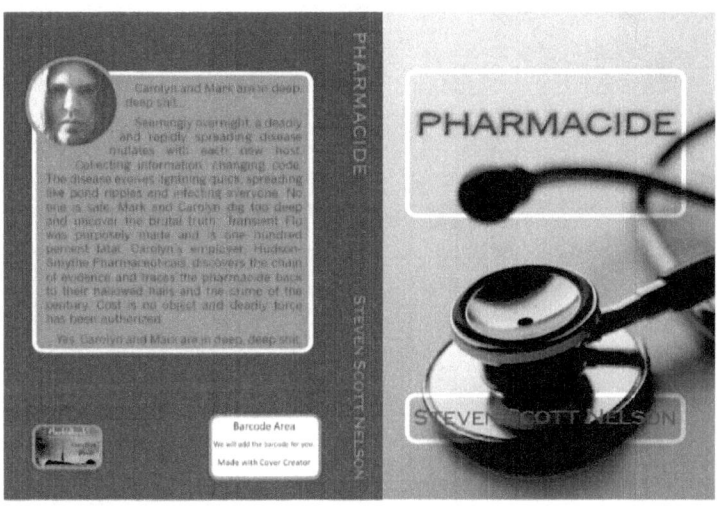

~It looks like Carolyn and Mark are in deep, deep shit... Mark
and Carolyn live in an alternate 1989 where Ronald Reagan is on
his fourth presidential term. The USA has a rigid, long-standing
caste system and abortions were never made legal. Being
homeless is a crime that is punishable by imprisonment in Tent
City. Most of Mark's ER patients are inmates at this camp and are
victims of a new disease dubbed. Transient Flu. This deadly and
rapidly spreading disease mutates with each new host, collecting
information, changing code. The disease evolves lightning quick,
spreading like pond ripples...

~IMMANUEL THE CHRIST has some nerve. Jonah has already lost everyone he loves to Pilate the vampire and his Harbor drug violence. Jonah now trudges through his days staying as high on Plata as possible. He just wants to be left alone while he waits for his turn to die. The Christ has other plans for him. She sends Pedro, to assign Jonah to order the Herod to dismantle the Harbor's Plata trade. Jonah decides to run. But you can't run from God. As Jonah learns the hard way when the 'Edmund Fitzgerald' goes down in rough seas, with the reluctant prophet on board...

~**Five Very Wicked Shorts.** Brought to you with love and blood from The Grim Reverend Steven Rage, the 'Most Depraved Writer in Print'. ~

Through the sheer shock of his presentation, Rage forces readers to consider the alternatives, to look at the garbage in the streets, to see what is swept into the gutters at night right before all decent people awake to see another cleaned up version of the day. Depravity at its finest, but really the stories are loads of fun.

~**Pontius Pilate is cursed to be a vampire**. Life after life after life.~ And for the Plata dealing Pilate, his life is more like a death sentence. His only chance surviving is to keep on selling his monthly quota of Plata. This new man-made narcotic is a potent speed-ball designed to amp up the user, while also numbing the conscience into euphoric oblivion. To nullify the pain. To stifle the torture. To run and to hid from all the anguish inside. PILATE is a drug lord vampire in this re-telling of Christ's final days.

~So I, The Spun Monkey, have returned from running my errands, safe and sound. Having failed rehab once again, The Spun Monkey went ahead and procured myself an 8-ball of crispy, crunchy Columbian Bam-Bam. I chipped, chopped, lined and blasted off with two bigguns up each side. OOH OOH EEE EEE-fuckmerunning- OOH-OOH-OOH, motherfuckers! Monkey be ready... Yes, indeeeeeed.... Having had my jet fuel, I then sat my hairy asshole down at the keyboard and began flailing away. The monkey hopes you dig the fruits of my labors in 'The Spun Monkey's Digest'. And if you not ... well then ... you can go eff yourself, Capitan!

~**Following religious folklore, parables, and beliefs,** Rage presents the readers with a God who truly is the Shepherd that leaves no sheep behind. While this tale is deeply woven with the intricacies of a dark, drug-infested world ruled by evil forces, this is the story of a lost sheep. All are God's children, even the most foulest of evil creatures who by their own will have become so through their spiritual and physical copulation with the Devil, and as such, in God's mercy, still are given a chance to be saved.

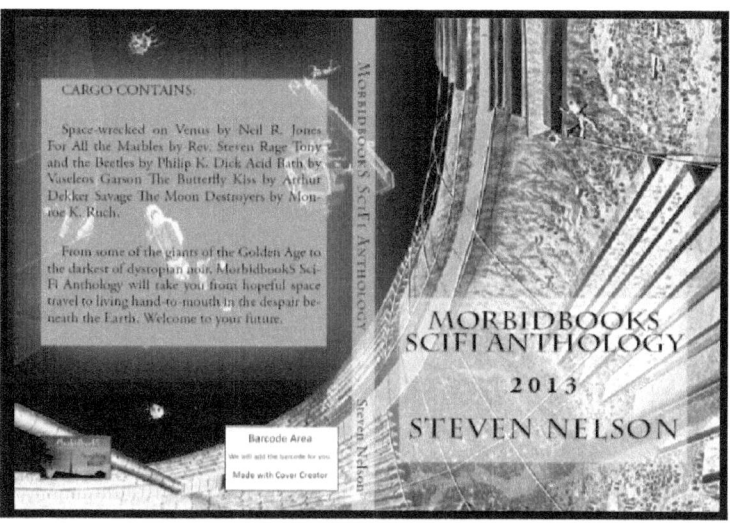

~ CARGO CONTAINS: ~

Space-wrecked on Venus by Neil R. Jones

For All the Marbles by Rev. Steven Rage

Tony and the Beetles by Philip K. Dick

Acid Bath by Vaseleos Garson

The Butterfly Kiss by Arthur Dekker Savage

The Moon Destroyers by Monroe K. Ruch

From some of the giants of the Golden Age to the darkest of dystopian noir, MorbidbookS SciFi Anthology will take you from hopeful space travel to living hand-to-mouth in the despair beneath the Earth.

Welcome to your future.

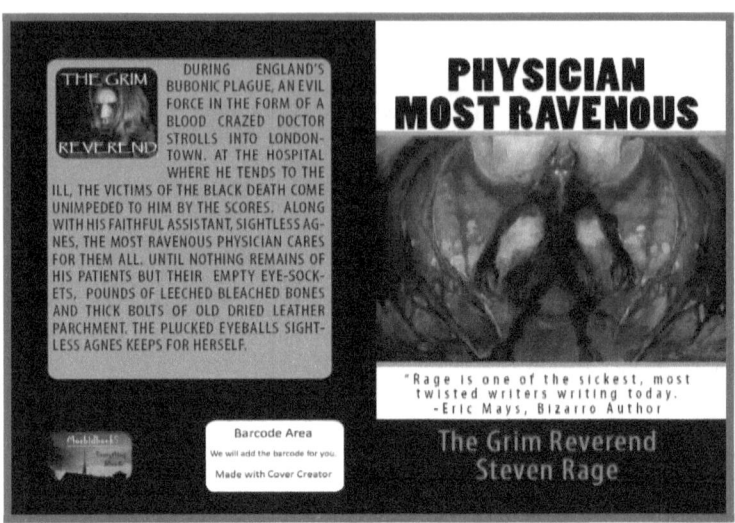

~During the height of England's Bubonic Plague an ancient Evil Force strolls into London-Town in the form of a would-be doctor. It could smell the blood from miles away, wanting only to help. At the hospital where he cares for the victims of this Black Death, the ill come to him unimpeded. They arrived and fell by the scores. With the help of his ever-faithful assistant, Sightless Agnes, a most ravenous cares for them all. Eating his way through an entire hospital, he treats them until there is nothing left. Nothing save their empty eye sockets, a few pounds of leeched bleached bones and some bolts of old dried-out flesh-leather parchment.

~**New from MorbidbookS: Where Everything Bleeds** is an instant collector's specimen and a certain stunner. ~ Be the first freak on your block to acquire this singular and unexpurgated exquisite culling of The Grim Reverend Steven Rage's favorite 'meds'. Enjoy this one-of-a-kind vivid look into the twisted mind of The Most Depraved Writer In Print as he captains you through the intoxicating stain of his wicked imagination. Included are numerous Photos, Paintings and Illustrations embellished with dramatic grayscale that enhance these iniquitous and magnificent Dark Fantasy fables.

MorbidbookS. Everything Bleeds.